Dedication

For my wife, who keeps my dreams alive.

For my daughter, who inspires me to dream bigger.

For my dog, who farts in her sleep.

The Sister-in-Law

AJ Carter

Papyrus

Copyright © 2023 by Papyrus Publishing LTD.
All rights reserved. No part of this publication may be reproduced, distributed, or transmitted in any form or by any means, including photocopying, recording, or other electronic or mechanical methods, without the prior written permission of the publisher, except in the case of brief quotations embodied in critical reviews and certain other non-commercial uses permitted by copyright law. For permission requests, write to the publisher, addressed "Attention: Permissions Coordinator," at the address below.

papyrusbooksuk@gmail.com

The Sister-in-Law

by AJ Carter

Prologue

I never truly thought it would go this far.

From the beginning, it was obvious I shouldn't trust her. Nobody wanted to listen – they all made excuses for her as if she were a child who hadn't yet figured out how the world works. But at the end of the day, trouble is trouble.

Especially when you're about to lose everything.

I'm backed into the corner of my own kitchen. My eyes are closed tight because I don't want to see what happens next. If only there was something I could do about the screaming – my baby being taken away from me while I'm trapped by a psychopath.

All I can think about is how wrong I've been. I

should have flown out of there the second I learned the truth about her, but hindsight is twenty-twenty. How was I supposed to know those little things could lead to something this bad?

How could I have known my life would end?

Chapter 1
Louise

Lisa is watching me. She knows I have something on my mind, but she's too polite to bring it up in front of all the other people from our coffee morning. She's been waiting for everyone to leave, and they're barely out of the café before she flings the question at me.

'What's winding you up so tight?'

I shrug, wrestling with the baby on my lap. Mia has just turned one, and she's usually very docile. Maybe all the goos and gaas from the other mums flipped a switch inside her because now it's like trying to restrain an octopus. I eventually give up and sit her back in the pram with a snack, desperate to keep her quiet while I spill the beans on what's bothering me.

'It's Daniel,' I say, reaching for my cold latte now that my hands are free. After taking a sip, I nurse it while tapping my fingers nervously against the white china. 'His sister is coming to stay with us, and I don't even know how long for.'

Lisa frowns. 'Is that a problem?'

'It is when you haven't met her before.'

'Oh, so she's practically a stranger?'

I nod, take another sip, then anxiously look over my shoulder at the door as another patron comes in for their morning fuel. It's starting to get busier in here, the queue reaching the door while spoons clink around in mugs and the coffee machine hisses and grinds. It smells amazing, but something is making me jittery and off balance. It could be the caffeine.

It could be the sister-in-law.

'She's just got out of prison,' I explain to the one woman in our weekly groups who doesn't have a baby. I'm not even sure why I'm telling her this – we've probably only had three or four conversations in our entire lives, but I have to tell *someone*. 'Their parents died a long time ago, and she doesn't have any friends, so she wants to stay in our guest bedroom until she's on her feet. It feels a little intrusive.'

'I can imagine. Especially with a little one in the house.'

'Exactly. And she's a criminal.'

'What did she do?'

'Vehicular manslaughter. Daniel was there the night it happened, and apparently, it was an honest mistake. She simply didn't see the other car coming, drove right into it, and killed the driver. It could happen to any one of us, I suppose.'

Lisa exhales and lowers her eyes to the table. 'Makes you think, doesn't it?'

I nod, but the truth is that I can only think about one thing: my husband's sister might not like me, and I might not even like her. From all the things he's said about her, she sounds like a wonderful person who just had a bad bit of luck. I actually feel a bit sorry for her, which undoubtedly had a hand in me agreeing to let her stay. I know it's normal to be slightly uncomfortable, but if things go wrong, then she'll just have to leave.

Daniel will have my back, like always.

'So, when are you meeting her?' Lisa asks.

'Today is the big day. I have to get back and clean the house, actually.'

'Finish your coffee first. I can tell you need to talk.'

It's nice to hear such selfless conversation from someone I barely know. Dolcester is such a small village hidden away in the north of England, and with only a thousand or so citizens, we should all know each other inside out by now. That's why I feel compelled to get it off my chest while I can. At least someone will know I'm struggling.

Following her instruction, I take two large gulps of latte and check on Mia. She's quite happy sitting there and focusing on the snack I gave her, eyeing it like it's the biggest conundrum this world has ever seen. It gives me enough time to ask one important thing.

'Should I be worried? About the sister-in-law, I mean.'

'I wouldn't have thought so. Is it the prison thing?'

'Yeah, I guess. It's not that I want to judge, but I hear that word and freak out.'

'Ah, but you trust your husband?'

'With my life.'

'Then trust him now. If he says she's a good person, why question it?'

She's right. It's far too soon to get my knickers in a twist. I should focus on meeting the woman before deciding if we made the right call. It's not like Daniel won't help me if things get awkward, so it's time to leave this café just as it's getting louder. I thank Lisa for the chat, then leave her behind while I start walking Mia home.

There's a big day ahead of us.

SOMETHING'S not quite right when we arrive home.

I've stopped at the end of our long drive, gazing up at the large Victorian house. It's a beautiful six-bedroom affair with the lushest greens surrounding the standalone building. My husband's salary as a doctor is the only reason we can afford this at all – I'm retired from writing for the local newspaper and am now on full-time baby duty. It's Tuesday, which means Daniel is working a seven-hour shift at the surgery.

So why is our front door open?

The mid-July sun is beating down on my back, luring me inside where it's usually cooler. I always try to keep a level head when there could be danger, so the first thing I do is call Daniel while keeping an eye on the house. Are we being burgled?

Daniel answers immediately, his pleasant voice singing down the phone.

'Hi, Louise. Everything okay?'

'You tell me. Our front door is open.'

'I had some leftover curry for lunch, so I'm airing the house.'

'Oh. You're home?'

Daniel laughs. 'Come inside. I can see you through the window.'

The call ends, and I turn my attention to the garage at the end of the drive. For security reasons, he always keeps the car inside. Daniel adores his beloved Jaguar, but locking it away when it's out of use always makes it hard to tell whether or not he's home. I sometimes wish he would keep it out on the drive.

Then we could avoid problems like this.

I tell myself it's no big deal, then carry on to the front door. Daniel meets me there, his thin body looking especially small in the wide doorway. Mia screams with joy as he leans in to kiss her, making all the appropriate noises to entertain a one-year-old. I love seeing these two together – it's the highlight of my day.

After helping us inside, Daniel pours me some water and starts cleaning up the kitchen. I sit Mia in her high chair and pull out some leftover lasagne from yesterday. She would've had curry, like us, but she hates the stuff. I set to feeding her, perching on the chair beside her.

'How come you're not at work?' I ask Daniel as he washes the dishes.

'There's not much to do today. The other doctor took the rest of my appointments.'

'Oh, that's nice.'

'Yeah, plus I get to be here when Abby arrives.'

I've been relieved for a couple of minutes now. I never did like the idea of meeting my sister-in-law on my own while juggling a baby. Now that Daniel is here, he can make the introductions and break the ice. That's a massive weight lifted.

'You've cleaned,' I say matter-of-factly, staring through to the living room.

'I didn't like the idea of you having to do it all. Especially as you have Mia.'

'Wow. Thank you. I was worried about not getting it done on time.'

'Well, now you don't have to.'

It's hard not to smile back at Daniel. Sure, he's evenly handsome, but his smile is nothing short of infectious. It's one of those bright, beaming ones that seems to extend to the rest of his features.

Better yet, I see it all the time. He always seems to be in a good mood.

'How are you feeling about seeing Abby?' I ask.

'A little nervous, actually. It's been six years.'

'I'm still astounded you didn't want to visit her in prison.'

'That was her choice, not mine. She didn't want me seeing her like that.'

'Which is fair enough.'

Daniel nods and drains the water, then dries his hands with a tea towel. 'How about you? Are you looking forward to meeting your new sister after all this time?'

I laugh and shake my head, but deep down, I'm terrified of making the wrong impression. Daniel has loved me since the day we met, coming on four years ago. We have our petty arguments just like any other couple, but we've never done anything to upset each other. If he ends up suspecting I don't like his sister, it will really rock this otherwise stable boat.

'I'm excited,' is all I tell him. 'Very, very excited.'

'You two will get along like a house on fire. Trust me.'

I want to trust him, but I've never been great

with people. My conversational skills aren't exactly up to scratch, so I tend to not say much. Unless the questions are about our baby girl, that is. Then you can't shut me up. I'm a proud mamma bear.

When Mia is finished eating and the final bit of tidying up is done, it's almost one o'clock. Abby is due to arrive any minute, and I'm desperately on edge. It's taking all of my energy to hide the shakes in my hands, but I think Daniel catches on.

As always, he doesn't miss a thing.

'Everything all right?' he asks.

'I'm fine. Just tired.'

We put on the TV as a bit of quiet background noise, letting Mia sit on the carpet. She doesn't like the children's show too much and is far more interested in making a mess on our floor. I don't mind, really – it's not like we can hide the fact we have a baby in the house.

I start watching the clock. Daniel takes my hand but says nothing. The minute hand almost completes a revolution before the hour hand moves. Suddenly, it's half past two, and Abby is late. I wonder if her taxi driver got lost. It's painful because, while I'm waiting, this is the most anxious I've ever been in my life. I just want her to arrive already.

At least then I can breathe properly.

Daniel must know I'm on edge because he suggests I go for a nap. Mia is rubbing her eyes anyway, so it might not be the worst idea. The only concern I have is that I might not be awake when Abby arrives. That's a sure-fire way to leave a bad first impression.

'Are you sure?' I ask, biting my lower lip. 'What if she comes as soon as I go upstairs?'

'I could wake you if you like?'

'Won't she think I'm lazy or something?'

Daniel smirks and shakes his head. 'You seem to think she's a bad person just because she's been in prison. Trust me, she's very nice and will have no problem understanding that a tired mother needs to get some shut-eye.'

I convince myself that he's right. Abby is still a mystery to me, save for some photos of her as a teenager. She certainly didn't look like a criminal back then, but I've heard it a thousand times in books and films: "Prison changes you, man."

But he *is* right, and there's no need for me to fight my fatigue.

I take Mia upstairs and lay her in her cot. She falls asleep instantly, so I take the baby monitor with me and head into my own bedroom, crawling under the duvet while still in my clothes. There, I stare up at the ceiling while the fan breaks through the humid weather and puts a fresh breeze on my face. My mind is racing, leaving me worried that I'll miss Abby's arrival, and it's hard to get to sleep. Minutes roll by, which turns into almost an hour, and then my eyes finally start to close. I immediately dream of Abby turning up at our house. She's asking where I am and calling me rude for not waiting on her even longer.

Suddenly, it feels like a nightmare.

Chapter 2
Daniel

I CAN TELL Louise is worrying, but I really don't want her to. There's a little solace in the fact she'll soon meet my sister, and all her troubles will be over. In my mind, there's no way in hell these two halves of my world can't merge easily.

Louise and Abby are the two best people I know.

The house feels empty when my wife is upstairs. Mia is asleep, too, which means I have to tread lightly as I pace this enormous house. I feel lucky to have such a place and to share it with those I love. Abby is going to lose it when she sees how well I'm doing, but the thought of her breaks my joy and makes me wonder where she is.

It's a whole hour before I get the call.

'Dr. Wright,' I say, answering the unknown number.

'Look at you, sounding all professional and stuff.'

I laugh at the sound of my sister's voice. It's so good to hear her after all this time. Until now, our communication has been limited to letters. I was starting to forget what she sounds like: sweet, fun, and excited to be out of her cage.

'Is everything okay?' I ask, glancing at my watch. 'You're an hour late.'

'Yeah, the taxi hasn't come.'

'Oh. You're still at the prison?'

'Standing outside on my tod, using a payphone.'

'In this baking heat? Tell me you have shade.'

'As a matter of fact, I don't. Which is why I need you.'

A small sigh escapes me. I'd do absolutely anything for my sister, especially given the circumstances. But with Louise taking a well-deserved rest and Mia asleep in her cot, it's not like I can leave the house. Waking them up isn't really an option either, as they both need their sleep. I'm completely and utterly lost.

'I'm not sure I can come and get you,' I say. 'Maybe I can order another taxi?'

'And make me wait even longer? Come on, I'm excited to see you.'

'But my baby is—'

'Ah, right. I forgot about the baby.'

The disappointment in her voice sounds so defeatist. I hate that I'm the one to make her feel like that, especially when this is such a big deal for her. Abandoning her outside the prison is hardly a great way to celebrate her release day.

'Let me see if I can get Mia into the car without waking her,' I say.

'Doesn't Louise have her?'

'Yes, but I want her to rest.'

'And what if the baby wakes?'

'Then she'll scream the house down, in which case Louise will wake up.'

'So you can meet me regardless of whether you succeed with the transfer?'

It's too hard not to laugh. Abby always had a manipulative way of backing me into a corner to get what she wanted. She was the same with Mum and Dad until they passed away, but they found it less funny than I ever did.

'All right, sit tight. I'll be with you as soon as possible.'

Abby makes a kissing sound and then hangs up. The time pressure looms over me, but I try to remain calm as I head upstairs and take Mia from her cot. She looks so peaceful that I feel cruel for moving her, but thankfully, I transfer her into the car with no problems. I then make sure I leave a text for Louise before bringing the engine to life.

Finally, it's time to reunite with my sister.

It's a fifty-minute drive to the prison. I've spent the whole time wondering what Abby looks like now. Has she aged horribly, looking forty when she's ten years younger than that? It could be that she hasn't aged a day. I'd give anything to be like that – to appear like I'm younger than thirty when the truth is I'm closer to middle age. I look it, too.

After five minutes of driving slowly around the block, I eventually find her sitting on a bench beside a disused bus stop, where I can just about see the shape of her face through the broken glass. I don't want to wake Mia just yet, so I refrain from leaning on my horn, opting to simply roll down my window and wave at her instead. When she gets up, she grabs a small cloth sack and runs giddily towards me.

I can't help but get out of the car to embrace her.

Abby bounds into my open arms, holding me tight. We hold each other close for an awfully long time, and then I step back to get a good look at her. She's starting to look her age, but she's wearing it well. Crow's feet are creasing up the corners of her eyes, and her hair is slightly frayed. From prison-grade shampoo, most likely. It feels like I walked through some kind of portal and met with an older version of her. Not that it changes a thing.

Neither of us can stop smiling.

'It's so good to see you,' I say, holding her head in my cupped hands.

'You, too, but can I have my face back?'

'Sorry.' I let go.

'Nice car, by the way.'

'Thanks. She's my pride and joy.'

'Speaking of joy, where's that precious baby girl of yours? I can't wait to meet her.'

'She's in the back, but she's sleeping.'

'Oh, wow. The whole way here?'

'She had a long morning with Louise, I think.'

Abby nods silently, then peers through the

glass with her hands tucked between her legs. She's grinning like that goofy little kid I grew up with, losing her sense at the sight of such an adorable baby. Maybe I'm biased, but I understand her swooning. Mia is perfect.

I put her bag in the boot and then climb into the driver's side. Abby slides in beside me, wanting to keep the window down so she can get some fresh air while I drive. I can't say I blame her – she's mostly only seen the inside for six years – but that doesn't stop the wind from waking Mia up. She stirs at first, then starts to scream, leaving me no option but to stop.

'Let me see if I can cheer her up,' Abby says, already exiting the car.

'Fine, but don't be upset if you can't. You're a stranger, after all.'

Much to my amazement, Abby operates the seat belt buckle and slides Mia out with no problem at all. Mia instantly settles as Abby makes fun noises at her, making her giggle. I'm watching from the front seat, twisting my body so hard I'll probably tear something. I've never seen anything like this. Mia doesn't usually like anyone except her own parents.

Time goes by, and we spend twenty minutes

sitting on the side of the road. I think about Louise and wonder why she hasn't replied yet. It could be that she's still sleeping, so there's probably nothing to worry about. We might even have time to grab a bite to eat.

'We should make a move,' I tell Abby. 'Are you hungry?'

'I've only had one hot meal a day for six years. What do you think?'

I smile and think about the nearest place to us. I'm sure I saw a Burger King along the way, so we'll have to drive a little bit before getting some food. It's not the most nourishing of cuisines, but convincing Abby to eat a juicy burger isn't going to be a challenge.

Getting her to put my baby down will be the hard part.

Our bellies are full when we arrive back home. There's a small bag of food for Louise that's gone cold, but she doesn't much like burgers anyway. Still, she might appreciate the gesture.

'Don't tell me you live here,' Abby says, leaning to gawk up at the house.

'Yes, I do. And now, so do you. For the time

being, anyway.' Upon the very mention of that, I finally notice there's something missing – something more than the small bag I put in the boot earlier on. 'Where's all your stuff?'

Abby crooks an eyebrow, a blonde ringlet of hair flopping over her eye. 'What do you mean? I already gave you the bag. You took it from me as soon as we saw each other.'

'You don't have any real luggage?'

'Why would I?'

'Oh, let's see... so you have some clothes to wear, maybe?'

Abby shrugs in the same carefree way she always did. She never was very materialistic, but this is taking it to a whole new level. What kind of thirty-year-old woman only has the clothes on her back? I make a mental note to take her shopping as soon as possible. It might make a nice welcome-home gift to go along with the free accommodation.

I park in the garage and start getting Mia out of the back, her cute little smile warming my heart. Abby climbs out and takes her bag, rushing outside and still staring up at the house like she can hardly believe it. I wonder for a minute if she might actually be proud of me for the home I've managed to buy – she can see I'm doing okay, after all.

We go inside, and her expression doesn't change. She dumps her bag at the bottom of the stairs in the main hall, then starts looking around. She disappears from view while I unstrap Mia from the carry chair, then re-emerges in the dining room doorway.

'This place is huge!' she yells.

I put my finger to her lips, then point up towards the bedroom.

'What?' she says.

'Try to keep your voice down. It looks like Louise is still sleeping.'

'Oh, yeah, right. I can't wait to meet her.'

A smile makes its way on to my lips as I lift Mia from the seat. She's getting big now, which is a worry to me as I'm really enjoying her at this age. I was always destined to become a dad, and I couldn't have chosen a better woman to share all this with. With the slightest bit of luck, my baby girl will grow up to be just like her mum.

My warm, comforting thoughts are disturbed by the buzzing of my phone in my pocket. I freeze, unsure if I can reach my pocket. Abby comes to the rescue, taking her niece into her arms and making her smile all over again. As I leave the room to take the call, I wish Louise would have been awake to see this. Her natural bond with Mia is nothing short of amazing.

'Dr. Wright,' I say, putting the phone to my ear.

'Sorry to disturb you, but I need a favour.'

I close my eyes at the sound of my receptionist's voice. Ethel has been working with me for a whole year now, and she's great. The only problem is she never hesitates to ask when she needs someone looking over her shoulder.

'Go on,' I say with great reluctance.

'Remember when you asked me to start uploading some of the old patient files digitally? Well, I started this morning and made some really good progress, but then I must have pushed a button and lost it all.'

'All of it? How can...?' I take a deep breath. 'Are you sure it's all gone?'

'Not exactly. That's why I need you to come and check.'

'Can't Dr. Phillips help you?'

'He tried, but he can't make head or tail of it.'

I'm trying my hardest not to groan. It's not Ethel's fault, but she's the seventy-one-year-old who stubbornly refuses to retire. She doesn't get along with computers, but this equal opportunities system in the NHS kind of has me in a corner. I like the woman – I really do – but I wish she could be more technologically minded.

The thought crosses my mind that I could tell her I'm busy and it will just have to wait. I'm supposed to be working today anyway, however, and another thought does occur to me. I ask Ethel if she can hold the line while I figure this out, then return to Abby. She's lifting Mia into the air like a rocket ship and making her giggle.

'Abby, I need your help,' I say, trying to disguise my displeasure at the uncomfortable position I've been put in. 'Someone at the surgery really needs me, and she can't find anyone else. Seeing as you're getting on so well with Mia, would you mind—?'

'You don't even need to finish that sentence. I'm here for you.'

'Thank you so much. If Louise wakes up—'

'I'll try not to disturb her.'

'You're the best.'

'I know.'

Once I'm back on the phone, I grab my car keys and tell Ethel I'm on my way. I really don't like the idea of leaving Abby alone with her, but it's clear she knows what she's doing. She's my sister, after all, and I trust her with my life.

I even trust her with Mia's.

Chapter 3
Louise

I awake with a start, my sense of time completely askew. It feels like I've come out of a coma after many long years, a foul taste in my mouth and my back aching from the foetal position I've been in all this time. How long was I out, I wonder, catching a glimpse of my messy brown hair in the mirror across the room? Why hasn't Daniel woken me?

It must be because I clearly needed the rest. Daniel has always been good at making sure I get to relax, so I smile to myself as I reach for my phone. There are two text messages there: one saying he's gone to pick up Abby and the other asking if I want food.

I don't.

Putting my phone back into my pocket, I check the baby monitor. There's no sign of Mia on the screen, which checks out. But over the whir of the fan in my room, I swear there's noise coming from the nursery. I hit the button on the fan and turn it off with a clunking sound. The blades slow down, dying as the sound of gentle humming comes from the monitor.

What on earth is going on?

I crank up the volume to hear it. It's a soft voice, a lullaby I vaguely recognise. I stare at the screen, waiting for answers as a chill creeps up my spine. Is somebody in the house? Have they taken Mia and fled, all while Daniel is on a short road trip?

The question answers itself as someone appears on-screen. All I see is the side profile of someone in jeans and a tight shirt. The voice and brief glimpse of feminine curves give away that it's a woman. But what concerns me isn't just the stranger in our house.

It's the fact she's holding my baby.

I leap from the bed and into the hall, my bare feet slapping against the wooden floor. I've never been any version of brave, but my own safety is no longer a priority while someone is in the nursery.

There's no point in creeping around, tiptoeing so the woman doesn't hear me. I'm just running, the adrenaline shocking me out of my sleepy haze.

The door bursts open and hits the wall. Mia starts screaming at the noise. The woman turns around, and I'm ready to pounce on her if she doesn't put down my little girl. Only it doesn't get that far because, as she turns to look at me, I see an older version of the teenager in the photos. The same facial structure, only tainted by the cruelty of age.

I realise I've just met Abby.

'You must be Louise,' she says with a kind smile.

My heart is still racing, the stress of Mia's wails ringing like an alarm through my entire body. I step forward and take her into my arms. Abby doesn't protest, simply stepping back and letting me take over. My instincts kick in so easily, patting Mia's bottom and gently stroking the back of her neck. That always seems to calm her. Her screams simmer into infrequent hiccups of tears, and then she's calm as I sway her in my arms.

'Bomb diffused,' I say, my blood still bubbling through me.

'Good job. Sorry if I scared you.'

'No, it's not your fault. Where's Daniel?'

'He had to run out to work real quick. I'm a bit in the deep end with babies.'

I can feel myself frowning at the fact Daniel did that. It's fine that he trusts his sister, but surely he must realise that I don't even know her yet. That she's a total stranger to me. Even now, while we're standing in the same room only metres apart, I don't really know anything about her. So was it really wise to leave her with our daughter?

'Why don't you meet me downstairs?' I say, calm but firm. 'Give us a chance to recover from what just happened, then we can start afresh over a pot of coffee.'

'Good idea.' Abby smiles. 'Want me to start making it?'

'If you know how to operate a coffee machine, that sounds good.'

'I'll figure it out.'

She practically skips out the door like a little girl. My first impression of her wasn't great, but it was hardly her fault. I blame Daniel for leaving her with a baby on the same day she got out of prison. No wonder Mia was screaming so loud – she likely read the stress in the room and endeavoured to match it. As for Abby... I'm not sure. She needs a real chance.

I stay in the nursery for a few more minutes, calming both Mia and myself, then make my way downstairs. The aromatic and enticing smell of coffee is emanating from the kitchen. As I enter the room with Mia in my arms, I spot a Burger King bag on the dining table and a pot of coffee in the middle, with two mugs laid out. Abby has used our special china from my wedding, but I try not to let it bother me.

'When is Daniel due back?' I ask.

'I'm not sure. He said he wouldn't be long, but that was two hours ago.'

'Yeah, work keeps him busy. One of only two doctors in the village and all that.'

'Makes sense. Are we all calmed down now?' she asks, taking a seat.

'I certainly hope so.' We both laugh at the unease as I lower Mia into her high chair and give her a slice of melon from the fridge. She quietly eats it while I take a deep, steadying breath and sit across from Abby. 'So... hi. I'm Louise.'

'I'm Abby,' she says. Then: 'You're not exactly how I imagined you.'

'Oh?'

'For some reason, I pictured a blonde.'

I laugh nervously. 'Why's that?'

'Daniel has always been more into blondes, so there must be something special about you for him to settle. With that said, have you thought about dying your hair? It might make him more attracted to you.'

I'm stunned. Speechless. Not only is she very direct, but I happen to think she's being rather rude. Has Daniel said he's not attracted to me? Have they had a conversation about me behind my back? If he has, it's left me feeling very uncomfortable.

'Daniel likes my hair.'

'Really?'

'Yes, really. He tells me every day.'

'Are you sure?'

'Of course I'm sure. Why is it so surprising?'

'Like I said, you're not exactly Daniel's type.'

The kitchen goes quiet, with just the sound of Mia's happy chewing filling the silence. Meanwhile, Abby and I stare off at each other. I hope this isn't how it's going to be – a battle of insults. I don't want to lower myself to her level of rudeness, but I can't help mentioning the one thing that would put her in her place. I have to let her know this is my home.

'How was prison?' I ask, trying not to smirk.

'It was exactly as you can imagine. I think the TV shows do it justice, if you're into that sort of stuff. It's very orderly, with a lot of bad things going on behind the scenes.' She bats away my question with such grace, as if she's not ashamed of what happened. Her response actually helps bring down the aggression in the room, easing me somewhat. 'It's a shame to have missed out on so much though. Like your wedding, for instance. And the birth of your little ray of sunshine. Those are moments I won't get a second chance at, you know?'

I nod politely and reach for my coffee, adding milk from the small pot Abby has filled from the fridge. I don't drink it just yet because I'm worried the caffeine will just agitate me more. I want to get on with my sister-in-law – I really do – and I'm going to keep trying.

'So, do you have a plan for the rest of your life? Have you thought about a job?'

'Absolutely. I'll just take some time to settle in and then get straight to work anywhere I can find it. Until then, I'm really sorry to take up space in your family home. It must be quite an intrusion, so thank you very much for letting me stay here.'

'You're very welcome. It's not like we don't have the space.'

'I just want you to know it's not gone unappreciated.'

This is more like it. This is the Abby I wanted to meet in the first place. It feels like our little struggle for power has been shoved aside, and now I'm presented with a woman I can get on with. I start to relax, finally taking a sip of coffee while thinking of something else to say.

It turns out I don't need to – Daniel is pulling up on the drive, returning from work and saving us from awkward conversation. I hear the garage door open and shut, then him trudging through the gravel before the front door opens. Abby gets up, putting a hand on my shoulder. She leans in close and whispers something in my ear.

'Here he is,' she says. 'Maybe next time, don't fall asleep when meeting your sister-in-law, okay? It's very rude, and I expected better of you.'

The words are long out of her mouth before I register what she just said. By then, she's striding out of the room and making a beeline for Daniel.

They hug as he gets in the door, and I quickly realise that this is the happiest I've ever seen him.

Suddenly, I feel a shiver on my arms.

My home is no longer a comfort.

'Ah, I see the two of you have finally met,' Daniel says, entering the kitchen. He distributes kisses to his wife and daughter, then takes a mug from the cupboard and pours himself a coffee. He doesn't sit because he can't – Abby is glued to his hip. 'How are you guys getting on?'

'Absolutely fine,' Abby says before I can answer. 'Isn't that right, Louise?'

I want to tell him. That I'm trying really hard to get along with her. That she's – if you'll allow me to be frank – pretty damn horrible. But she's his sister, and I want him to know there's nothing to worry about at home. Not when his work is stressful enough.

They each take a seat after I've nodded, hiding my grimace behind my coffee mug. Daniel reaches for my hand while staring lovingly into my eyes. Abby is a picture of happiness, sighing with pride as she watches the two of us interact.

'It's so nice to see you happy, bro,' she says.

'Why wouldn't I be happy? I'm the luckiest man in the world.'

'That's what I was just saying to Louise. You have a lovely wife.'

I almost spit out my coffee at her sudden personality transplant. Only moments ago, she was doing everything in her power to start an argument – throwing a handful of digs my way and seeing what stuck. I refused to bite. I'm too busy raising a kid to get involved in squabbles.

'Do we have any plans for the week?' I ask Daniel, moving the conversation along.

'Yes, actually. I've booked tomorrow off so we can go shopping.'

'Into the city?'

'No. It's market day tomorrow, and Abby needs some clothes.'

Of course, I totally forgot. On the first Wednesday of every month, the central road in our small village is closed, transforming the usually mundane street into a wealth of colours and noise. The whole village comes to life, shopping for cheap goods and fresh groceries and some even enjoying treats from food vans. Daniel and I have a ritual of eating one of their cheesy hot dogs. The problem is, this year, I just don't feel like eating crap.

'That would be really nice,' Abby says merrily. 'Louise, would you come with us?'

I try not to raise an eyebrow at her because it's not a case of me going with them – it should be *her* coming with *us*. 'Yes, I'm coming. It might be a nice bonding experience.'

'Are you sure? If you're too tired...'

'I'm fine.'

Abby shrugs. Daniels smiles, completely oblivious to the psychological warfare his sister is trying to get off the ground. I wonder if this is how it's going to be the entire time – if I'd better get used to being second best while Abby is around. I certainly hope not because my marriage with Daniel is the one constantly sturdy thing in my life.

It would be a shame if someone came between us.

Chapter 4
Daniel

The very next day goes somewhat smoother. There's no rushing to get things clean, no worrying about what time Abby will arrive. I actually wake up in my bed after a solid night's sleep for once, then wake up knowing she's already here in my home.

It feels like a dream come true.

We're heading into the market today, and it's nice and easy getting ready. I'm one of those people who rushes through a shower and throws on any old shirt, so I take Mia and play with her a little while the ladies get ready to go out. It takes a little under an hour.

We share the same car, Louise cramped up with

the baby in the back while Abby sits up front with me. She stares out the window in amazement the whole way. It makes me realise this is her first time seeing Dolcester. She's admiring the range of expansive fields, the greenery popping under the July sun. By the time we reach the main village, she's making sounds at the cobblestone streets and Victorian-style homes like she's impressed. To think, she was always locked up only a few short miles from here.

She never got to see the quaint beauty of this place.

I park the Jaguar at the far end of the car park, lowering the odds of someone scratching the paint. We all climb out, unfold Mia's buggy from the boot, then head towards the entrance of the market. The place is buzzing with life, the smell of cooking meat drifting over on the summer breeze. Kids are running around with candyfloss, yelling with excitement as they chase each other. It reminds me of being a kid myself. Abby is right here beside me.

'What shall we do first?' I ask the gang. 'Shopping or eating?'

'I was thinking about grabbing something for Mia,' Louise says.

'Yeah, but I'm starving,' Abby announces like it's the most important thing in the world.

I glance over at Louise, who rolls her eyes, then shrugs. I don't know what's got into her, but she suddenly seems far less interested in being here. That shrug speaks a thousand words, chiefly among which is that we should part ways for the time being.

'Let's split up,' I say, taking control. 'Louise, do you want to get started on the Mia thing? Abby and I can do some shopping for clothes, then we can meet in the square in half an hour?'

'Don't you want to stick together?' she asks.

'I don't want to be a problem,' Abby claims. 'Let's do it Louise's way.'

We all look at each other, and I'd be lying if I said it wasn't annoying to be pulled in different directions. I make the snap decision after reading all their expressions. 'Let's just do what I said before. Is that okay with everyone?'

Abby nods. Louise hesitates, then does the same. She doesn't speak another word, turning the buggy around and wheeling it towards the far end of the market, where large groups and families are heading in. Abby looks at me like she's worried she's done something wrong.

'It's fine,' I tell her, slinging an arm around her shoulder. 'Let's go have some fun.'

It's NOT easy to forget that Abby is an ex-convict, but the village folk seem to manage. Between the car park and the second row of market stalls alone, over five people have stopped to talk to me, each of them over the moon to finally meet the good doctor's sister.

Abby has already stressed that she's worried people won't like her, instantly labelling her as a bad apple due to her car incident a few years back. She seems to react well, all things considered. She shakes hands with people, greeting them with a warm smile while they fuss over her. It's amazing: she's instantly a part of the village.

When we finally get a chance to look at some clothes, I take a step back and allow her to pick out things she wants. I really am hopeless when it comes to wardrobe fashion, but that doesn't stop her from showing me the occasional item, holding things up against her body and asking me what I think. I say all there really is to say.

'It's very nice.'

Abby laughs at my awkwardness, then moves

on, creating a physical wish list before stopping at a near-empty table to pick out the bits she wants. She has to narrow it down to just a couple of things, she says, because she doesn't want to take advantage.

'It's not taking advantage,' I tell her. 'Remember, I'm the one offering you money.'

'But you're already doing so much by letting me stay with you.'

'You're my sister, so you deserve the very best. Let me buy it all.'

'Daniel—'

'I insist.'

She shoots me a look that's half gratitude, half defeat, but it doesn't stop her from taking all of the clothes to the market seller and waiting to hear the total cost. It's not that much – a mere £120 for six whole wardrobe changes – but I can tell it means the world to her.

As we move on, we bump into Louise. She's hiding something, rushing to tuck it under Mia's buggy. I suspect it's something to do with my birthday, which is just around the corner, so I pretend I don't see, opening her up to approach us when she's ready.

'I think I've got all I need,' she says with a smile. But that smile fades as she looks at the massive brown paper bag in Abby's hands. 'You must have bought a lot of clothes. I didn't think you'd need much space, so I'll need to make more room in your wardrobe.'

'That's okay,' Abby tells her. 'I can fold it up and put it on the floor.'

'Really, it's not a problem.'

'But you're getting flustered by making a fuss over me.'

I have to intervene. 'I'll find you some space. For now, why don't we move along?'

Louise shakes her head. 'I'd like to put something back in the car. Can I borrow the keys? I'll bring them right back to you when we meet for food.'

Abby doesn't say a word, but I can see she's suspicious of my wife. I'll explain it to her in a second, but for now, I simply hand the car keys to Louise and watch her head back the way we came. My giddy stare is interrupted by Abby placing the heavy bag in my hand.

'Help a lady out,' she says.

'Who said you're a lady?'

'Ha ha.'

She hits me on the arm a little too hard, but I pay it no mind. How can I when it's so glaringly obvious something is wrong? Abby has always been full of life, a sparkle behind her eyes at all times. She's had that same look since I picked her up yesterday, but after seeing Louise, her entire character seems to have taken a negative turn.

'Is something wrong?' I ask, arranging the bag in my hand.

'No. Well, maybe. It's nothing.'

'Hey, it's not nothing. If it's bothering you, then out with it.'

Abby bites her lip as if she's making the biggest decision of her life. I'm already starting to worry – she deserves a second chance after what happened to her that night in the car. I wait patiently while she gathers the courage to say it.

'Can we sit? I'm getting a little shaky.'

'You need to just tell me what's wrong.'

'Please, let's just sit down first. Louise will be back any minute.'

Struggling to find the right words, I just nod and lead her in the direction of the benches near the food stalls. It won't be long before Louise catches up to us, so whatever needs to be talked about should be done as fast as possible. I'm just wondering how bad it is.

I really hope it's nothing serious.

. . .

WE FIND room in the shade between two burger vans, the smell making me hungry. I can't even think about food right now, though, because Abby needs my help with something that's apparently time sensitive. I sit down on a picnic bench out of the blazing sun. She quickly joins me, keeping an eye on the crowd. Presumably so she can see Louise coming.

'Want to tell me what's going on?' I ask.

'Yeah, I... Does Louise like me?'

I can't help but hesitate because this question came completely out of the blue. 'Of course she likes you. Why wouldn't she?'

Abby wipes something out from under her eye. It's not clear whether it's a drop of sweat or the start of a tear. Either way, she doesn't look at me. 'She's been rude to me ever since I got here, but only when you're not around.'

'Rude like how?'

'Well, she snatched Mia out of my arms when we first met.'

'To be fair, she didn't know you.'

'True, but she didn't have to call me a bitch.'

'She *what*?'

'Yeah, she told me I have no right to be here. I should get my own damn house, she said.'

I can barely believe what I'm hearing. Louise has never been the type of person to speak to others that way, but she certainly has been acting strange since we decided Abby would come to stay. I wonder if she feels threatened by my sister. Perhaps my attention has been somewhat divided lately, but that doesn't give her the right to talk to my family like that.

To be honest, if it wasn't Abby telling me this, then I wouldn't believe it at all. But I know a liar when I see one, and that's not her. If she says somebody called her a nasty name or has been rude to her, it's more than likely true.

'What else has she done?' I ask tentatively.

'She mentioned something about how I take up too much space.'

'Are you sure that's what she said?'

'Positive. That's why I felt so uncomfortable when she mentioned the clothes.'

Now that I think about it, something was a little off about that conversation. The things Abby tells me are starting to gain a little credit because I know when people are uncomfortable, and that was definitely a tense interaction. I'm also good at telling when people are scared – I've delivered bad news to many patients in my time, and they all give off the same signals. Everything from wringing their fingers to avoiding eye contact.

The same things Abby is doing right now.

'I'll talk to her,' I say because I don't know what else to do.

'Don't do it on my account. I was just figuring out why she hates me.'

'She really doesn't hate you.'

'It feels like it.'

Before I can say any more, Louise emerges from the crowd with Mia in the buggy, who points at me with the biggest grin on her face. It's amazing to see her so happy, and if I wasn't already put in a bad mood from this recent bombshell, I would be feeling on top of the world.

'Have you eaten yet?' Louise asks, looking over at the burger vans.

Abby shakes her head and then slides on a pair of sunglasses. You could cut the tension with a knife, and it's causing me to sweat even more than the sweltering sun is. All I want is for my sister and wife to get on for the short duration of Abby's stay, but that seems like a sad implausibility. At least without intervention.

It seems like the day is ruined, but we might as well eat while we're here. We each get a burger and chips with a can of fizzy drink, while Mia eats small parts from each of our portions. I'm doing my best to keep the conversation flowing, and Louise is taking it as casually as always. But I can tell something is wrong. Maybe she knows Abby has told me those things, or maybe she's so oblivious to her actions that she thinks everything is just fine.

But I know when my sister is upset. It's so clear in the way she shrinks back from conversation, doing all she can to stay out of harm's way like a stray cat avoiding traffic. She doesn't need to feel that way. Not any more – not when she's with me.

I need to have words with Louise.

Chapter 5
Louise

It's a grim day.

The heatwave seems to have ended overnight, casting the north of England in grey, murky clouds. A slight drizzle sprinkles against our windows with shy tapping sounds, but the weather isn't the problem. Today, I have other hardships.

It starts as soon as I wake up after a long, haunting dream about the market yesterday. I had a nightmare that I couldn't find Daniel. I searched and searched through the growing crowd, calling his name, but to no avail. Mia was in my arms the whole time, and even she was screaming for her dad, although she can't talk yet in the real world. When I did eventually find him, he was getting in a car with Abby, deciding to spend the rest of his life with his old family rather than the one he'd built from scratch.

I woke up in a sweat, and that was that.

It's put me in a bad mood, but I'm trying not to look too far into it. Instead, I focus on the here and now, checking the baby monitor to see Mia isn't in her cot. As Daniel is downstairs – I can hear him playing in a childlike tone – she must be safe with him in the living room. I throw on some clothes, run a brush through my hair, then make my way downstairs.

Everyone is up before me. Abby is drinking coffee in Daniel's favourite chair, while my husband is throwing Mia slightly into the air and catching her. Mia loves it, cackling like she can't breathe as the laughter takes her. It makes me laugh, too, until they get too close to my parents' urns on the mantelpiece. Mia knocks one. My father's. It wobbles, and time stands still. The room goes quiet in dreaded anticipation until it comes to rest.

'Maybe play closer to the centre of the room,' I say, going to say hi to my daughter.

But Daniel stops me there, wiping beads of sweat off his forehead with the back of his hand. 'Actually, before we start the day, I'd like to talk to you about something. Can we go in the kitchen for a moment? It's important.'

Abby doesn't look at me, so I wonder if it's about her. We leave Mia with Abby and go into the kitchen, where I instantly pour myself a coffee, realise it's all been used up, then sigh and get to making another pot. Today is already off to a bad start.

'Do you not like Abby?' Daniels asks bluntly.

I'm taken aback, the weighty question shocking me awake better than coffee ever could.

'What?' I say. 'Why do you ask?'

'She thinks you have something against her. Apparently, you've been nasty to her since the moment she arrived.'

'That's a lie.'

'Is it?'

'Of course it is.' I put down the coffee pot without turning it on, then go to him. My hands reach out to take his, but he pulls away, leaving me with nothing to do but frown at this ridiculousness. 'I'm not really sure where this has come from. In fact, she's the one who—'

'I don't want to play games, Louise. Did you, or did you not, call her a bitch?'

I can barely believe what I'm hearing. Is this

what Abby is doing behind my back? Causing trouble where it doesn't need to be caused? I was already doing my best not to argue with her after those snide comments, but this is insanity.

'No, of course I didn't call her a bitch. Why would I?'

'I don't know. Maybe you think she's taking up too much space.'

'What are you talking about?'

'So, you're denying that as well?'

'What? Yes!'

Daniel huffs an exasperated breath and then rubs his eyes with the heels of his hands. It's the same stressed look I see after a long day's work. I just never thought I would be the cause of it. Or, more accurately, *Abby* would be the cause.

'Look,' I say, cutting through the mystery. 'I don't know what she's been saying to you, but I've only been nice to her. We had a bit of a rough start when I woke up to find her holding Mia – remember, she was still a stranger to me, so I was in shock – but I thought we got things back on track pretty quickly. This is all such nonsense.'

'Well, she doesn't think it is. She's really upset.'

'Okay.' I take a minute to breathe. To focus. 'All right. Clearly there's been a miscommunication somewhere. Would it help if I went in right now and spoke to her?'

'Yes, that would really help.'

'Okay. Could you take Mia while I do that?'

'Sure.'

Daniel is calming down, but I can tell he's still irate as we head back into the living room. He scoops Mia up off the floor without a word, then returns to the kitchen. Now I'm alone with Abby and a huge mess to clear up. I have to choose my words carefully, otherwise it's going to cause an even bigger rift between me and Daniel.

It's been a long time since I've been this nervous.

Before I can get out a single word, Abby stands and turns her back on me. She goes to the window as if I don't exist, watching the rain as it patters against the glass. She's waiting for me to speak, making a power play that I can't be bothered to compete with.

'Why did you tell Daniel I called you a bitch?' I say, cutting to the chase.

Abby doesn't say so much as a word, but she does turn around and look at me.

'Well?'

'You did.'

'We both know I didn't.'

'Then I must have been hearing things. Or you just don't remember.'

'Abby, my memory isn't so bad that I'd forget calling *anyone* that.'

'Are you sure? You are almost forty, after all. Maybe that's affecting your recall.'

My mouth drops open. I can't believe what I'm hearing. I spin my head around to see if Daniel heard any of that, but he's feeding Mia in the next room, doing his best impersonation of a plane like he usually does with the spoon. I'm truly lost for words.

Abby takes a slow, confident stroll around the room, looking at photos on the walls. 'It doesn't have to be like this, you know. We could be friends.'

'That's what I've wanted this whole time.'

'Then why can't you just be nice to me?'

'Can you give me an example of how I'm not being nice?'

'It's just in your tone. You don't like me. It's obvious.'

'I don't yet have an opinion of you one way or the other, but I definitely don't hate you.' Abby starts to make her way to the mantelpiece, where she studies the urns and then reaches out to touch one. 'Please don't. Those are my parents'.'

To be fair to her, Abby respects this and withdraws a hand. But her gaze still fixes on them. 'Your mum and dad? What happened to them?'

'They both died from cancer in the same year.'

'Ouch. That sucks.'

'Yes, it does.'

Abby turns around, but she lingers by the urns, looking right at me. 'Obviously, something has been misconstrued somewhere along the line. Maybe we can start afresh. We're all spending the day together again, so there's no point in making it difficult.'

'Agreed.' I extend a hand. 'Fresh start as friends?'

'Better than that.' Abby shakes my hand, gently and warmly. 'Family.'

I breathe a sigh of relief, hoping to sweep all of this under the rug. It was never my intention to upset her, and I hoped that was clear from the fact I never reported her sly comments to Daniel. But I like the fact she's offered to wipe the slate clean. Maybe now we can build a relationship – become friends or family, or whatever she wants.

'I'd better go take over with Mia's food. See you in a bit?'

'Definitely.'

The smile Abby gives me is so kind and genuine that it's hard not to like her. Now in a more positive frame of mind, I go into the kitchen and see Mia making a mess with her porridge. I start to smile, my affections for her overwhelming every one of my senses.

Until I hear a sound that fills me with dreaded disbelief.

It's a sharp, shattering sound. I freeze on the spot, my brain taking a moment to catch up to what's happening. In my mind's eye, I search around the living room, thinking of all the things that could've broken. When I piece together that Abby was standing by the urns and they're made of ceramic, my entire body fills with adrenaline.

Suddenly, my good mood is plummeting back down.

All I feel is panic.

The moment I enter the living room, my heart crumbles.

The urns have been smashed to pieces. Both of them. The ceramic covers the floor like thrown confetti, the remains of my parents coating the hardwood floor like dust. I can't breathe. My pulse is racing. My blood is boiling. I can't even bring myself to look at Abby, who's standing beside the fireplace with her hands clapped to her shocked cheeks.

'What's going on in...? Oh.'

Daniel appears beside me with Mia in his arms, but they seem to float by like it's some kind of bad dream. I'm still frozen, unable to believe what I'm seeing in front of me. Has this really happened? Has Abby really destroyed my mum's and dad's urns?

'It was an accident, I swear!' Abby protests.

Her voice is barely more than a muffle to me because all I feel in my ears is a rush of blood. This is the first time I've ever wanted to hit someone, and if Mia wasn't in the room to witness such violence, I would already be slapping Abby.

'God, this is terrible,' Daniel says, looking around. 'Erm...'

He puts Mia down in her playpen in the corner of the room, then starts sifting through the ashes to pick out parts of the broken urns. I still can't bring myself to move because I can't trust myself not to lunge at my godawful sister-in-law.

'Louise?' Daniel says. 'Louise, are you listening?'

I slowly emerge from my daze, turning to my husband.

'Can you go and get a pot, a clean tea towel, and the vacuum?'

'I'm not about to hoover up my parents!'

'Relax. That's what the cloth is for. Trust me.'

'I'll get those things,' Abby says, rushing out of the room. 'I'm so sorry. I really didn't mean to do that. It was an accident, Louise. I promise.'

I pay her no mind, somehow finding my way to the sofa so I can sit down. If I don't, it's quite possible that I'll faint. It seems like only seconds before Abby comes back. I watch with morbid anticipation as Daniel puts the towel over the vacuum nozzle, blasts it on and then uses the suction to escort the ashes into the new pot. I feel sick, a funny taste sitting on my tongue like I'm going to throw up. I still might.

Within just a few minutes, the ashes are all cleared up, save for the remaining thin layer on the floor. Daniel informs me that there's no option but to sweep that up and have done with it, advising me to leave the room while he finishes the job. I know he's doing the right thing, and I'm ever so grateful for him handling the situation, but this still feels so wrong.

My mum and dad don't belong in the bin.

I get up to leave. Abby tells me again how sorry she is, insisting she didn't intend to destroy the urns. Daniel sides with her, telling her it's okay and that accidents happen. I wish he could see what I see – how vindictive his little sister is. Maybe then he might believe me if I tell him the truth about what Abby is doing as I leave the room with my heart in pieces – the look she's giving me while he has his back turned. I can barely believe it myself, but it's clear as day and impossible to deny.

She's grinning.

Chapter 6
The Watcher

She begins the day as she always does, crawling out of bed with her brain feeling too big for her skull. The hangover rages inside her head, her stomach feeling like a shaken bottle of Coke. There's only one solution to this beat-up sensation she endures most mornings, which is to crawl out of her bed and grab a beer from the fridge.

There, in the dark, she sits and contemplates life. There isn't much to hers, most of it spent inside this cheap, dusty old flat in a block that nobody comes near unless they're as poor as she is, returning home after a night on the town. But for the Watcher, this is a place of solitude. Of quiet contemplation and to engage the ghosts that haunt her.

It keeps coming back to her: the face on that woman. The confident, cocky sneer that's lodged in her memory for good. She takes a long, desperate sip of beer and shakes the thought away, instead letting her eyes drift down to her belly. It's not bloated like it should be – the alcohol is taking its toll by now – but instead, she's painfully skinny because she supplements her food with pure misery and nothing else.

This is her life now, and she must suffer it.

The clock says it's midday. It's time to sit at her computer and ignore the outside world. There's a wealth of nostalgic distractions, looking up friends from her past to see they're now married and have kids. She looks up the shut-down nightclub she used to frequent, now defaced with graffiti and used by junkies to shoot up in private. The Watcher hates seeing this – the setting of her youth has been treated worse than she has.

And they all know how bad things were for *her*.

She continues to browse, slowly emptying the beer between her unbrushed teeth. There's a smell coming off her, but who cares? It's not like she's going anywhere or seeing anyone. It's just her, the computer, and a certain news article that makes her drop the beer.

As she reads the headline, her pulse quickens. She's glad she's sitting down because it would have surely made her fall. The horrors of what happened come back to her as she reads and then rereads each line, the mugshot of her demon staring back at her as if to taunt her – as if daring her to remember every detail of what wrecked her life. She can barely believe what she's seeing, her heart beating a rapid rhythm while she searches for ways to accept the truth.

That Abby Wright is a free woman.

Chapter 7
Daniel

It takes far too long to get the ashes off the floor. I'm doing everything I can to ensure Louise doesn't see what I'm doing. It's bad enough this has happened at all, but she shouldn't have to watch as her parents are cleaned up off the floor.

Abby is standing nearby, and I feel just as bad for her as I do for my own wife. The poor thing was already worried that Louise doesn't like her, and now that she's made one fatally clumsy mistake, it's only going to make matters worse.

A little over an hour after the incident, I have the ashes gathered into a single pot. There's obviously no way I can separate the two of them, but perhaps this tragedy could be twisted to look somewhat romantic. My in-laws loved each other dearly – that's what I hear, though I never did get to meet them – and now their remains are entwined for all eternity. Not that there's anything dignified about being kept in a pot, but I'll fix that this afternoon.

It's safe to say our plans are cancelled.

I start looking for a safe, temporary place to keep the pot, opting for the very top of the kitchen cupboard. I'll head out in a while to find a replacement urn – I have a rough idea of who might be able to help – but first, I have to run damage control. There's not a doubt in my mind that this disaster has caused rocky waters between my wife and sister. If I can do anything at all to reduce the tension between them, I'll do it.

Abby is looking after Mia in the living room, so I search the house for Louise. I find her upstairs, lying on our marital bed in the foetal position. There are soft sniffles coming from her, but she's buried her face in her hands. I step inside to ask if she's okay.

'I want to be alone right now,' she says.

The smart thing to do is respect that, so I tell her I'm here if she needs anything, then step outside. I think about reminding her that Abby didn't mean to knock over the urns, but she wouldn't believe me anyway. No good can come from opening my mouth.

Heading back downstairs, I see Abby sitting on the floor. Mia is on her lap, and a book is open between the two of them. Abby is reading aloud to her, putting on a happy, bubbly voice to make my daughter laugh. But there's no fooling me. I know when my own sister is feeling awful, and I really feel for her. She shouldn't have to hide her own emotions.

'Can we talk?' I ask.

Mia looks up with a happy grin, but I don't want her hearing this. It doesn't matter that she doesn't quite understand words yet, but there's a certain vibe that comes with emotionally charged conversations. If she picks up on that, she may not always be the happy little girl we were fortunate enough to be given.

Abby nods, finishes the book with her own made-up ending, and then I put Mia in her pen. We go to the hallway, but I linger in the door so I can keep an eye on Mia. Our voices are reduced to hushed whispers, separating my baby from the negativity.

'Louise is really upset,' I tell Abby. 'You should go and talk to her.'

'Is that really such a good idea? She hates me enough as it is.'

'Exactly. A heartfelt apology could go a long way.'

'If you think so. I don't know if...'

Something strange happens then. My sister, who I've only seen cry a small handful of times in my entire life, suddenly has the first crystallising shine of tears in her eyes. She tries to hide it, but I see it coming and put a hand on her shoulder.

'What's wrong?'

'You just don't understand what it's like. I spent six years in prison, where everyone hates each other. I even hate myself for what I did. But then I come out thinking things will be different, like such things don't exist in the outside world. Then the first thing I see is Louise treating me terribly, and now this happens, and I don't know if I can face it. It's too hard, Daniel. It's just too hard!'

I pull her into my chest and hold her tight, letting her know I'm here for her. It really wasn't her fault that she went to prison – I was there the night of the accident, and that's exactly what it was: an accident. It wrecked the lives of those who knew the victim, but it also ruined Abby's. Now she has a chance to truly live and make up for the years spent behind bars... and she's already reduced to tears? It doesn't seem fair to me, but I'm not about to say it aloud.

All I can do is comfort her.

An hour or so after that heartbreaking moment, I need to head into town for a replacement urn. Louise is hardly in a fit state to take care of a baby, and Abby is particularly sensitive right now, so I separate the two by taking Abby with me.

Very little is spoken during the short journey into Dolcester, but not much needs to be said. I now know how Abby is feeling, and believe me when I say I'd do anything to take that misery away from her. I don't communicate that thought either, but she knows. How can she not, after so many years of being her number-one guardian?

I stop the car in the car park of the village's only supermarket. A friend of mine lives nearby, and I'm hoping it'll be a quick in-and-out, so I ask Abby to watch Mia while I quickly head two streets over and bang on Roger's door.

Roger is a good man who used to run a funeral

home back in the day. He's retired now, living out his remaining years in a small one-bedroom house that's just big enough for his needs. Besides, he spends a lot of time out fishing on the lake, so home comforts mean very little to him. How do I know this? Like I said, he's a friend. He confides in me, and I do the same. Call it a bonding of professions; I patch people up to improve their lives, while he prepares them for death. At least, he used to.

'Daniel,' he says, smiling thinly through his yellow-white beard. 'What brings you here?'

'Hi, Roger. I need a favour.'

'Anything for you. Come on in.'

I step inside but don't go too far in as I don't want to intrude on his private life. It smells like an old person's home should, if that person neglects his health and hygiene. To be completely honest, it smells like something died in here.

'I won't take up much of your time,' I say, stuffing my hands in my pockets. 'We had a bit of an incident this morning regarding my in-laws' urns. You don't happen to have a spare one lying around from your old business?'

'An incident?' He frowns, his face suddenly gaining more wrinkles and creases. 'It happens more than you'd think, Doc. Let me have a look for you. Would you like a cup of tea while you wait? I think I saw some biscuits in the cupboard a few days ago, too.'

'No, thanks. Just the urn.'

'It might take some time.'

'I can wait.'

Roger disappears into the dark house, leaving me to linger in the hall. The smell is disturbing, and there's a mess – boxes stacked to head height and growing mould – but I'm grateful to be out of the weird tug of war that the sun and rain clouds are playing. I simply wait until Roger comes back with a very basic but somewhat beautiful urn that's comprised of both metal and oak. He hands it to me, and I wonder if it will be big enough.

'That's the only one I could find, so I hope it does the job.'

'It's perfect, thank you.'

'How's that wife of yours?'

'She's fine,' I lie. 'She says hello.'

'Tell her hello back. I also hear your sister has come to stay?'

'Yes, she's in the car now. I'd best be off.'

I thank him again and rush back to the car

park, cradling the urn in my arms. It's heavier than I thought it would be, but maybe that's a good thing. Not only would it be harder to knock off a mantelpiece if such an accident should occur again, but it might not even break after it falls. It looks good, too. It's not the gorgeously patterned ceramic Louise picked out for her parents before we met, but it'll do.

I just hope she appreciates the effort.

Abby takes Mia into the garden when we return, making use of the sun having dried up all the rain. There's a calming glow in the blue sky as the clouds drift far into the distance. It's a good thing they're fleeing the scene at last. They were starting to remind me of ashes.

I get to work on the urn right away, very carefully transferring the remains from the pot and into the urn. The lid has a seal on it that activates with a button press and a fierce twist. It brings me comfort to know her parents will be safe in this. It's not exactly what they would have wanted, but I did the best I could from a bad situation.

When I head into the living room to put it above the fireplace, Louise is standing there by the window. She's dressed down into a gown and turns to watch me, pale-faced and miserable. I love this woman – I really do – but it's getting hard to juggle the emotions of both her and my sister. But at least I've been trying, as represented by the urn I place on the mantle.

'What happened?' Louise asks, almost desperately.

'I went into town to get this from Roger.'

'The funeral director?'

'Ex. But yes.'

She shuffles towards me, studies it at great length, then plants a kiss on my cheek. A tear transfers from her face to mine. It's still warm. Definitely fresh. 'Thank you,' she says. 'But we really need to talk about Abby.'

'Why don't you try talking *to* her instead?'

'Because she's not reasonable.'

I sigh, then go to the window myself and stare out at our long, beautiful lawn. It's hard to be upset when you spend your day-to-day life in a house this grand, but somehow, it's happened. All three of us are slowly losing our minds. 'There's absolutely nothing wrong with my sister. You just need to get to know her a bit.'

'That's what I'm trying to do, but she hates me.'

'She thinks it's the other way around.'

'Obviously, I don't love her after she knocked the urns over.'

'Come on, you know that was an accident.'

She comes up behind me and turns me around, then cups my cheeks in her hands. She's still pale, almost ghostly, piercing me with her greyish-green eyes. 'I'm not just pointing fingers here, but look at that fireplace. It's really difficult to knock even one thing off the mantle. It's so high up and out of the way. How could it have been an accident?'

I look at it just like she requested, and I admit it would be hard, but the alternative is even more preposterous. 'You're right. It would be hard to knock something off, but what else could have happened? Why would she do that on purpose?'

'You tell me. You're the one who knows her.'

'Which is why I find it so hard to believe.'

'But she smirked at me, Daniel. As soon as your back was turned, she actually grinned.'

'Now you're being ridiculous.'

Louise huffs and walks away from me. It feels like she's about to perform a demonstration of what happened, but she just goes further and further away until she's out the door. I wait for a while, thinking she'll bring something in to argue her case, but then I hear the creaks and groans of the mattress in our room as she climbs back into bed.

I guess Abby and I are taking care of Mia today.

Chapter 8
Louise

Now that I've had some time to calm down, it's safe for me to return to my mothering duties. I feel bad for ever having let my emotions get the better of me, especially when it directly impacted my relationship with my daughter. I feel as though I've disgraced myself.

But that doesn't mean my thoughts have no credibility.

Abby definitely grinned at me two days ago, after knocking the urns on to the floor. I just can't get my head around what might make a person do something like that. Does she really despise me so much that she would go to such lengths to upset me? What have I done to make her feel so hateful? Worse yet, is it possible I'm seeing things – that she really didn't smile behind Daniel's back and my exhausted mind is just filling in the blanks?

These are all thoughts I take with me into town. Daniel is back at work today after the surgery begged him to come back in. He didn't like it one bit, but it's his job, and he didn't have much of a choice. I do, however, and when facing the idea of being stuck alone in a house with Abby all day, I decide I'm badly in need of advice.

The coffee mums are all waiting for me outside the café, gathering in the shade on this particularly hot day. They're as confused about the English weather as I am, as evidenced by the mixture of T-shirts, dresses, and hoodies. Nonetheless, they all seem happy to see me when I take a seat at their table and order a decaff using the app.

What happens next is nothing out of the ordinary. We all sit in a circle and go over ten or fifteen minutes of mindless rambling about whatever we've seen on TV, what miniscule developments our children have made in the past couple of days, and how much sleep we did or didn't get last night. When the time comes to finally address my issue – that's the reason we're meeting, after all – I'm well-prepared to tell my side of the story.

They all listen politely, their kids wriggling on

their laps as the mothers hold them in place with steady hands. Their stunned expressions are all the same, and I imagine that's what my own face looked like back when Abby desecrated my parents' remains.

'You need to make her leave the house,' one of them says.

'It was probably an accident,' says another.

Two more agree with the latter, but Lisa is shaking her head.

'If one thing is dead clear, it's that she's making herself the boss in your own house and disrespecting you. Daniel might hate you for doing it, but if you don't take a stand and let her know she's pushing her luck, she'll walk all over you. She's had her chance.'

It's weird how the other mums are suddenly backing up her advice. The table becomes a sea of nodding and mumbled agreement. I trust Lisa enough to know she's probably right, but the advice is best suited for someone a little more... territorial. I never was the kind of person to put my foot down and dictate how things should be done. That said, I know what's at stake.

'What if she tells me to go walk off a cliff?' I ask. 'Daniel will defend her regardless.'

'Then you can do the same to him,' Lisa says, laughing. 'Seriously, you're acting like the house belongs to him and you're just another guest, like his sister is. Most of the money came from him, but is the house half yours or not?'

'Well, yeah, but—'

'Then grow a spine.'

The other mums keep nodding. I hate that they're encouraging me to be more abrasive, but they're probably right. Whether or not Abby is deliberately messing with my head, she needs to be made aware of how she's behaving... and what will happen if she doesn't change.

We spend the rest of the morning having a laugh about less serious matters, and everyone seems to leave one person at a time over a span of around fifteen minutes. Lisa and I are the last ones yet again, and as soon as we're alone, she leans in closer to me.

'I didn't want to say it in front of the other ladies, but you need to be careful.'

I sit and bite my tongue, with Mia asleep but starting to stir against my beating heart.

'I've met people like Abby before. They're all the same; they cause trouble, cry when things don't go their way, then lower their heads when they're confronted. But one thing is always the same, no matter who it is.'

'What's that?' I ask, anxious anticipation bubbling inside me.

Lisa leans in closer still. 'They're all aggressive when threatened.'

I'M TOO scared to go home. All I can think about is what Abby might be doing or thinking. I imagine her sitting in my living room, probably in my favourite seat, drinking from my favourite mug while deleting my favourite recorded shows off the TV. I've villainised her in my head... or has she done that to herself?

Regardless of who's to blame, action needs to be taken. Mia is sleeping in her buggy, so I take the long route home, walking through the long, meandering lanes behind back gardens. It's hardly the most scenic route, but right now, thinking space is far more important than something pretty to look at. Anyway, there are fewer things to wake Mia up this way.

By the time I get halfway home, I've already decided what needs to be done. Lisa was right, but she was also very wrong. There's nothing wrong with puffing my chest out and letting Abby know who's boss, but that doesn't mean I have to be cruel about it. I'm going to have some very firm words with her, letting her know how I feel and telling her things have to change. Is it too much to demand respect in my own home?

When I do finally make it back to the house, I'm dripping with sweat from the mid-afternoon sun. I'm parched, my lips dry and cracking. Mia stirs as I manoeuvre the buggy through the front door, finding her a nice spot in the kitchen where the sun isn't too bright.

Then I hear footsteps.

I highly doubt it's Daniel, as I know he's out to work at the moment. As if to prove my suspicions, Abby walks into the kitchen and goes straight for the fridge, drinking milk out of the bottle without so much as an acknowledgement. When she finishes – putting the bottle back, which I hate with a passion but keep to myself – she closes the fridge door, glances at Mia, then looks at me with quiet contemplation.

Until she speaks.

'You're soaked. Did someone hose you down?'

'It's sweat,' I tell her. 'It's really hot out there.'

'Hmm. You should have been more prepared.'

With that, she leaves the room with her chin up, humming a tune that makes Mia's eyes slowly start to open. I'm already sick to death of Abby, and that last comment didn't help. I now have a very limited window in which I can address the issue before Mia's fully awake, so I gather my wits and head after her.

That's my first mistake.

ABBY KEEPS WALKING LONG after I call her name. I feel stupid as I follow close behind her, asking if we can have a minute alone but then being completely ignored. I stubbornly keep following her, saying her name over and over until we reach the guest bedroom.

Then she slams the door in my face.

I feel humiliated. Furious, even. There's such disrespect coming from her that I don't know how to handle this any more. The only thing I know for sure is that I can't go in and speak to her because Mia has started making gentle sobbing noises in the kitchen. I go to her, swearing under my breath just to let out a fraction of the anger I feel.

After that, I'm watching the clock until Daniel comes home. He's not due until after six o'clock, and I have nothing to do but play games with Mia, putting on some music and dancing like a loony. Over time, it even starts to cheer me up, my problems melting away, if only for a short while. My life is temporarily bliss.

A little after five, Abby emerges from the guest room. She makes her presence known by humming merrily, as if nothing has happened between us at all since the day she got here. She coos at Mia, who beams with excitement at the very sight of her, then disappears into the kitchen once more. I must admit, I'm a little worked up that my daughter seems to like her because I'm coming closer and closer to realising she's a real piece of work.

Abby is rustling in the kitchen, going through my snack cupboard without even asking if it's okay. My blood is boiling more as the day goes on, to the point I've now decided to prevent her retreat back to the bedroom. I put Mia down, then stand in the doorway and block Abby's path when she finally tries to come back through.

'Oh, please move,' she says, sounding so annoyingly calm.

'In a moment. First, we need to talk.'

It took everything I have to even say that much to her, but my confidence is instantly shot down by the condescending smirk on her face. She crooks an eyebrow, then places a hand on her hip. Her eyes go to the small gap between my arm and the door frame, like she's thinking of rushing into her little cave, but I move my body to block it further.

'We don't need to talk,' she says so matter-of-factly. 'You just need to sit down.'

'I'll sit down when you explain why you're behaving this way.'

'What way?'

'You have to be joking,' I scoff. 'Talking to me how you do, knocking my parents' urns over, telling Daniel lies about the way I've been acting towards you. You've been an absolute nightmare to me, Abby, and it's going to end right now. If not, you'll have to—'

My words are physically cut off when she shoots out a hand. It clamps around my throat, making me gag. With a sudden display of strength, she forces me back into the hallway, pinning me against the wall as I freeze in utter shock.

'Let me make one thing clear to you,' she says, hissing through her clenched teeth. Now her eyes are wide and alive with more ire than I've ever seen in my life. They're the eyes of a convict – a tougher woman than myself, who would do anything to get what she wants. 'You may think you're in charge here, but you're not. You're nothing but a useless tart who happened to catch the eye of my big brother. *I'm* in charge. Don't believe me? Ask him.'

I can barely breathe. Even as her grip loosens ever so slightly, my sheer terror has me holding my breath, the tension cutting off my basic survival instincts. I'm not even doing anything with my hands – I'm simply too afraid to fight back.

'Mama,' Mia calls, sounding lost and alone in the other room.

Abby cranes her neck towards the doorway, sees that my baby is witnessing such an awful scene, then let's go. As I catch my breath, she leans in close and leaves her final comment. 'I'm staying here for as long as I like, so you better get used to it. Face it, wench. I own you.'

She gives me one last shove before blowing a kiss to Mia. Mia smiles and makes a cute smitten sound, and then Abby disappears up the hall and into her room. I'm still standing here, stunned and unable to think straight as I wonder just how on earth I'm supposed to tell Daniel about this. He wouldn't believe me, and it's not like I can prove it anyway. Which means I'm in an even worse situation than before because now it's official.

Abby is staying in my home whether I like it or not.

And there's not a damn thing I can do about it.

Chapter 9
Daniel

I GET HOME TOO late tonight, my work snowing me under as it sometimes does. It feels like I'm being punished for taking a couple of days off, but I have no regrets. Abby needed welcoming to our home, and I'd do it again if I had to.

By the time I get inside and kick off my shoes, the whole house has gone to bed. It's eerily quiet, the only light coming from a lamp in the hallway that Louise always leaves on for me when she knows I'm working late. I smile as always, rub my tired eyes, then make a quick snack before bed. I'm not too hungry – my worries about Abby and Louise are affecting my appetite. I just can't seem to shake the whole situation from my mind.

Louise is sleeping soundly when I come into the

bedroom, so I check Mia is okay on the monitor, then strip down and join my wife. I fall asleep instantly, waking up what seems like minutes later to the sun rising. It's been a dreamless night, but I slept soundly. That's exhaustion getting the better of me, I suppose.

I find Louise downstairs as I slip on my suit jacket. She's nursing a cup of coffee while watching the portable monitor. Mia hasn't stirred yet, which means we have a couple of minutes before I get an early start, which, hopefully, means an early finish.

Except Louise has a face like thunder.

'Morning,' I say, reaching for an apple from the bowl. 'You all right?'

'Not really. You'd better sit down for this.'

I don't know what to expect, but my senses are on high alert. If this is going to be about another tiff between her and Abby, I don't want to hear it. Sometimes it feels like there are three children living under my roof, and Mia is the most mature of them all.

Hesitantly, I sit.

'Your sister is causing problems,' she says outright, nervously tapping her mug. 'Ever since she first arrived, she's been driving a wedge between the two of us, acting one way when you're around and then changing completely as soon as you leave the room.'

'If this is about the urns—'

'It's not. Yesterday, she grabbed me by the throat.'

Anger is rising from my belly, but I'm somehow able to hold it back... a little. 'Listen, if you don't like her, that's one thing, but I've known Abby my whole life, and there's not a chance in hell she would do that to anyone.'

'Oh, really. The vehicular manslaughterer wouldn't hurt a fly?'

'That's not fair. You know it was an accident. That's why it's called manslaughter.'

'You're missing the point.' She pushes her mug aside and points down at the table as though she's taking a stand. 'I just told you that your sister has physically assaulted your wife, and you don't seem to give a damn.'

'Because you're lying!'

It slips from my mouth, and I'll never forget the way Louise is looking at me. It's a wide-eyed expression of shock, with a little bit of misery sprinkled in. I can tell she can't believe I just said that, but it's the truth. Abby would never lay a hand on another human being.

Never.

Louise doesn't wait for more. Seeming to accept it's a lost cause, she shoves her chair back as the legs scratch the tiles, then storms out of the room with the baby monitor. I know she feels like she has a right to be angry, but so do I. It's already getting to me that these two aren't seeing eye to eye, but this is getting ridiculous. My wife is lying to me about something that didn't happen – *couldn't* happen – and I just don't see why she's doing this.

Does she hate Abby? Is that it? Or perhaps she's just jealous because she's not receiving every ounce of my attention for once. It's probably my own fault – I've been spoiling Louise since the day we met, and now she's become accustomed to it.

So I only have myself to blame, right?

No. I can't think like that. This whole thing is Louise's doing, and if she can't alter her attitude to at least *try* getting along with Abby, then I have no idea what else to do.

That's the situation she's put me in.

· · ·

A DAY at work almost seems like a holiday compared to the drama at home. It's a small, enclosed office with just enough room for the examination table and a large corner desk where I can spread out all of my files. There's plenty to do today – not nearly enough time to get it done – but I've hardly touched it.

All I can think about is Louise.

Now that I've cooled down a bit, I wonder if there might have been any truth to what she said. There's simply no way Abby grabbed my wife by the throat, but that story must have come from somewhere. Maybe it's an exaggeration built from something smaller. Maybe she did do it after all, but she was only being playful. It could even be that all she did was pat her shoulder, and my drama queen of a wife turned it into something it wasn't.

This is the most stressed I've been for a while, and I don't have anyone to talk to about it. Nobody is in the office today except for Ethel, who's managing the phones out in reception. She doesn't make much of a conversationalist anyway, so it's a case of keeping this burden to myself and praying it goes away.

That's when I get the idea.

Posting anonymously on the internet was never really my thing. I'm what they call 'a lurker'. I study posts from other people rather than spilling my own secrets where everyone can see them, but a long and thorough search brings up nothing. There is one post about how a lady doesn't get on with her new housemate, but it's mostly because of the mess she leaves.

It's not even similar.

Against my better judgement, I open up a window to ask fellow users of the website, and then I start typing. My fingers do the rest of the work, telling the whole story without me even having to think about how to phrase it. This makes me realise just how much it's been weighing me down, which only makes me angrier with Louise.

Why would she put this on me?

It's all typed out, so I give it a quick spellcheck and then hit the Publish button. Turning to my work to help pass the time, I actually manage to put it out of my mind for a short while, but then my browser starts blowing up with notifications. There are already over twenty replies, and more are coming through as I read them. They all say the same thing – mostly, anyway, but there are some toxic miscreants in the mix – and that is to say, I should ask Abby.

Of course, it's already crossed my mind. But to imagine for a moment that none of this has happened and that Louise has been causing trouble since the beginning... can I really ask Abby? She already thinks Louise hates her, and if she learns that a new lie has surfaced to incriminate her, it would probably destroy her.

I don't want to do that to my own sister.

But the internet folks are right.

I sigh as I finish reading and then shut the conversation down. The rest of the day drags by at a snail's pace. I can hardly concentrate on these files because all I can think about is the answers to my question and how right they are. Like it or not, I need to ask Abby.

Apparently, it's the right thing to do.

The end of the day comes right as the evening begins, which not only means I'm on time, but I'm about to come face to face with the problem that's been bugging me all day. After much long, hard contemplation, I've finally decided to ask Abby for her side of the story.

But the house is dead when I come in. There's no sign of anyone, and a subtle stab of concern pricks me. Has something serious happened between the two of them? I certainly hope not, and maybe they know better than to let things get out of hand.

Maybe.

The first thing I do is crack open a window and try not to panic because it's boiling inside the house. I then touch the radiator, quickly pulling away when the molten metal burns my hand. Why on earth is the heating on in the middle of summer? And where is everyone?

I turn the heating off immediately, then search the house from top to bottom. There's no sign of Louise, Mia, or the buggy, so it's safe to assume they went out somewhere. As for Abby, well, I find her in the guest bedroom with the door and windows wide open. She's sitting on the bed and watching a show on my tablet.

'Abby? What's going on?'

She looks up, pauses the show, then pushes the tablet away. 'What do you mean?'

'The house is empty. The heating is on full blast.'

'Oh. Louise turned it on before she went out for a walk.'

'Why?'

'Not sure. I did ask, but she just muttered something about it not being me who pays the bills.' She shrugs and then scoots to the end of the bed. Then she takes a second glance at me and easily guesses something is wrong. 'Why do you look all serious?'

'It's been a rough day.'

'Why don't you tell me about it?'

Abby pats the side of the bed, and I go to join her. This room in particular is like a furnace, as if Louise has been trying to smoke my sister out of the house. Even with the windows open, it feels like my skin is about to melt off. I'm sweating within seconds.

'Want to tell me what's wrong?' she asks.

'Yes and no.'

'Huh?'

'I mean, I *want* to tell you, but...' An exasperated sigh flees my mouth, freeing my lungs but not my conscience. It hurts that I have to go through with this, but it's only fair I hear both versions of yesterday's events. 'Did you strangle Louise?'

Abby stares at me, looking at my lips as though

they're about to clear up her confusion. She furrows her brow after a long wait, then lets out an awkward giggle. 'Is this a joke?'

'No, I'm dead serious.'

The giggle vanishes as quickly as the smile does. She's back to frowning in an instant. 'What? No, of course I didn't... Wait. I don't understand. Is this a metaphor or something?'

She's genuinely lost – nobody is that good an actress. She's as confused as I was when I first heard what happened, so I clarify everything by repeating what Louise said to me. The further in I get, the more worried she starts to look. By the time I reach the end, a single tear rolls down her cheek and hits the duvet.

'I don't understand why she keeps doing this to me,' she says, her voice cracking under the strain of more tears. 'She hates me so much, doesn't she? Why can't she just leave me alone and stop trying to turn you against me? One day, it might actually work.'

Sympathy wells up inside me. I reach an arm around her. She buries her face in my chest as she lets it all out – all the anguish caused by her own sister-in-law. Louise will undoubtedly get mad at the fact I'm siding with Abby, but I truly believe there wasn't an ounce of violence.

'I'm so sorry she's doing this,' I say, because it's all I *can* say.

'It's not you. It's her. I just want her to like me.'

'And she will. I promise.'

I have no idea how I'm going to keep that promise, but if there's one thing I do know, it's that I'm going to have some seriously harsh words with my wife. I'm done beating around the bush and listening to ridiculous lies. Louise needs to get her act together because all of this drama has put me at the end of my tether. I'm already starting to regret letting them meet.

Chapter 10
Louise

THERE WAS no way I was going to spend a day at home with Abby. I didn't feel safe, and why should I? She's already proven she has a mean streak by pinning me against the wall with her hand clamped around my throat. If that doesn't prove she's crazy, what does?

So I walked with Mia for as long as possible, getting plenty of air and stopping whenever one of us was hungry. I didn't go home until later tonight, skipping the family dinner and putting our baby girl straight to bed. Daniel came up later, wanting to talk, and I've ignored him ever since. Why bother when he's just going to take Abby's side?

I'm up most of the night, worrying about what's going to happen with me and my husband. Even when I do finally get to sleep, I'm startled awake by a panic-inducing dream about Abby mowing me down in a car I never knew she had. Then I lay awake for hours, thinking about her car accident and wondering... what if it unlocked a psychotic part of her? What if she never really recovered from the trauma of accidentally killing someone?

That dark thought is my only company throughout the night, but I do eventually fall asleep. The problem is, I'm awoken by Daniel after only a short while. He's perched on the side of the bed and lightly stroking my hair. I used to love it when he woke me like this, but now it feels like a stranger to me.

He's not the loyal, loving Daniel I used to know.

'Sorry to wake you, but we need to talk.'

Of course it's bad news. Why wouldn't it be? I rub my eyes and groan as I sit up, the world looking fuzzy as my exhausted eyes struggle to adjust to the daylight beaming through the open curtains. I steal a glance at the bedside clock – it's nine in the morning.

The baby monitor is off.

'Where's Mia?' I ask, sitting up instantly.

'Relax. She's with Abby.'

I hate this, but it's not like I'm allowed to say anything about it. Daniel has clearly chosen his allegiance, so my distaste for his psychotic sister is my own to bear. So I just nod, like a good, obedient wife who doesn't have a care in the world.

'What did you want to talk about?' I ask.

'Two things, actually. First, why did you put the heating on yesterday?'

'Sorry?' I shake my head, suddenly alert because I most definitely did not put the heating on. Abby did it – I saw her and even asked what she thought she was doing, but she just smiled thinly and then walked off. 'Did she tell you I turned it on?'

'Yes.'

'That sounds about right.' I sigh. 'What's the second thing?'

Daniel shakes his head. 'I'm worried about you, to be honest. Because now you're doing things without even realising. Anyway...' He takes a deep breath and blows it out with an exaggerated puff. 'You and Abby need to sort your problems out. Today.'

'Oh, we do? I suppose you didn't say the same thing to her?'

'No, and I'm not going to.'

'Can I ask why?'

'Because I've known her far longer than I've known you, and the things you're telling me don't even slightly align with who she is as a person. So, because of that, I want you on your feet and downstairs in ten minutes, ready to act like a real, loving sister-in-law.'

I blink the shock out of my eyes, but it does nothing. I didn't realise I was in a boot camp, and if I am, then I don't want to be here anyway. Much has changed since Daniel and I got married, but things only improved until a few days ago.

Until Abby got here.

I open my mouth to protest, but Daniel is already heading for the door. He lingers there for a minute with his back to me, then turns his head just to get out one final, devastating comment. 'If you don't fix this, we simply can't continue with this marriage.'

With that, he leaves the room with my heart in pieces.

When I do finally swallow my pride and head downstairs, the living room goes quiet. Mia screams happily at the sight of me and then crawls across the floor. I scoop her into my arms and start kissing all over her face to get a chuckle out of her, but I'm very aware of the awkwardness on the other side of the room.

Abby is sitting on the floor, surrounded by storybooks for babies, and now looking up at Daniel, who's standing nearby as if to oversee the scene. I feel like I'm on trial in my own home, and even though I resent the idea of going along with my husband's plan, there's little more to do than actually obey his orders.

Even if the word 'orders' does put a sickening taste in my mouth.

Their silent communication seems to last forever, only really breaking when Mia starts pointing at her father and signing for a drink. He hands her the bottle he's holding, and then I sit with her as she starts sucking on the rubber nozzle. I love seeing her happy, and judging by the longing expressions of adoration around the room, so does everyone else.

'I want to hold her,' Abby says, breaking the silence.

'Maybe in a minute,' I tell her. 'Let me say hello a little first.'

Abby then looks up at Daniel again, like a child

asking permission. I wonder if it's always been like this between the two of them – him taking on the big-brother act while she gets whatever the hell she wants just because Daniel loves her more than anything.

More than his wife, it seems.

'Let Abby hold her,' he tells me, giving me a dead stare to remind me of our conversation.

'She can,' I say calmly, feeling anything but. 'When I'm good and ready.'

'How about now, Louise?'

'It's okay,' Abby says. 'She's overprotective. That's normal.'

'It's definitely not okay.' Daniel steps forward, then leans into my ear as if nobody else in the room will hear it. 'Are you kidding me? We only just spoke about this. Try trusting her a little, or you'll never be friends with her.'

When he walks away, Abby is staring at me with lost but hopeful eyes. This is anything but the vicious ex-con who attacked me a couple of days ago. Is this the side of her Daniel always sees? Because it's so sickly sweet that I want to throw up in my mouth.

Now I have two options: do as Daniel tells me like an obedient little housewife or exercise the authority over my own child. Stubbornly, I take the latter and enforce the fact that I want a minute to ourselves before handing her off. I even tell her it's not personal.

As if she'll see it that way.

Daniel shoots me that look again – *'we simply can't continue with this marriage'* – that scares the ever-living hell out of me. I've never been the type to depend on others, but he's the love of my life and has always acted as such.

Until now.

I'll always hate myself for giving in. Mia is pulling towards Abby anyway, so it's no use fighting. I have to just resign and let her crawl across the carpet to see her auntie. God, it hurts just to think about the fact these two are related. And by blood, too.

Then, the unthinkable happens. Not only does Mia reach her estranged aunt, but she puts her head down on Abby's chest as if they're mother and daughter. I watch with absolute horror as my daughter shows her the affection I've always craved. Mia has never done that for me, so why should she do it for her godawful auntie after just a few days?

Daniel says, 'Aww.'

Abby tells her she loves her.

As for me? I'm the one person in the room who sees the way she's staring at me. Her face is concealed by the fierce hug from Mia, so she seizes advantage of this and sends a small smile my way. It's just enough to tell me that she's won, and whether I like it or not, she's going to keep collecting these little victories until I'm no longer relevant.

Even then, she'll keep rubbing it in my face because she was right all along.

She owns me.

There's no point in sticking around to take the provocation from Abby, so I leave the room and use the opportunity to take a break. Daniel is going to be at her side anyway, so it's not like our daughter is in immediate danger. Besides, one thing is clear.

Abby is only a threat to me.

I head for the bathroom, where I'm going to take a shower just to wash off some of this misery. The air is hot and humid, so it's refreshing to let the shower run cold and then stand under it for a long time. While I'm in here, I keep running recent events through my mind.

Why does Abby have to be so cruel? Why does she hate me when I've been nothing but nice to her? It seems as though she'll use any small chance to make me look like a problem. Take yesterday's heating problem, for example – she didn't need to do that at all.

My heart is still pounding with pure hate when I get out and dry myself off. I'm trying to distract myself by thinking of what our lives will be like just one year from now. Abby will be long gone, hopefully finding a job sooner rather than later. Then I follow that trail of thought, wondering if she's even bothered looking yet. Knowing her, probably not.

As soon as I'm dressed, I go downstairs to gulp a whole glass of orange juice, then make my way through to the living room to check on Mia. I'm already nervous about being in a room with Abby, but that only gets worse when I see her taking care of my daughter alone.

Daniel is nowhere to be seen.

'Is there a problem?' Abby asks, still sitting on the floor with my baby.

'Where's Daniel?'

'Cutting the grass. Why?'

I can hear it now – the very distant hum of

the ride-on lawnmower as it circles the grounds outside. It should be comforting that he's still nearby, but I hate that he's left her alone with Mia. Especially when he knows how uneasy I feel about her. It really goes to show how much he puts his own trust above my feelings as a whole.

'Never mind,' I say. 'I'd like to take Mia back now.'

'Mmm, no. She's quite okay where she is.'

A fleeting moment of courage lets me speak my mind. 'I'll decide that. I'm her mother.'

'Just like you're Daniel's wife, right?' Abby chortles to get a rise out of me. It's working. 'We'll just see how much he loves you when he has to choose between us. Because, let's be honest, it's not really looking in your favour, is it?'

I don't know what kind of game she's playing, but I've had enough. I stomp forward and reach for Mia. Abby moves her aside, just barely out of my reach. By then, I've lost all patience, so I step over her and grab my daughter under the arms. She screams at the unwelcome surprise, but I don't care much for her feelings when her safety is at risk. I pull her close to my chest, feeling the rough beat of her hands as she protests.

'Looks like *she* doesn't want you either,' Abby says.

I stifle my revulsion, summoning every ounce of self-control to not lash out at her in front of the baby. Mia starts to cry, so I take her out of the room and into the reading room at the back of the house. The crying turns to screaming, shrieking at the top of her lungs while I'm stuck with the threats Abby made.

Just who the hell does she think she is? Why can't I make my own husband believe the things she's saying? If the past few days have taught me anything, it's that I'll need concrete proof of the way she's behaving, and there's only one sure way to do that.

It's time to put up some cameras.

And catch her in the act.

Chapter 11
Daniel

I COME in from cutting the grass, and although I've not been doing it manually, the sweat is dripping off me with such intensity that it could fill buckets. I splash my face with cold, refreshing water and savour the shade inside the house, but we're out of tea towels to dry myself with. It's no big deal – they're probably drying in the reading room.

Right where I find Louise.

'Is everything all right?' I ask, instantly noticing her eyes are a little on the red side. Not that she'll look directly at me, but she never was very good at hiding these things.

'I'm fine,' she says. 'Just tired.'

'Why don't you go and have a nap?'

'Mia isn't ready for at least a couple more hours.'

Suddenly, I understand. It's why she's been so touchy lately and quite possibly why such gross paranoia has emerged in recent days. She's exhausted. How have I not seen that until now? I've been so busy trying to keep a balance between my work and family life that I never saw how hard my own wife was finding things.

She's been timing her days around Mia.

'Why don't you start worrying about *you* for once?'

'But what about Mia?'

'That's exactly my point.' I head closer inside and kneel next to her. She looks at me then, her eyes bloodshot through what could be a cocktail of deadly fatigue and – just maybe – the residue of a good cry. If there ever was such a thing as the latter. 'I'll take care of Mia. You just get yourself upstairs and have a good, solid sleep. No more deep thoughts for now, okay? Everything is taken care of.'

It's obvious she doesn't quite trust me with our child. More accurately, she doesn't trust Abby. But that will have to change at some point because we can't go on like this. Anyway, it's not like I'll leave her unsupervised.

After far too much contemplation, Louise finally decides to go upstairs. She has one last check on Mia – sneaking in a final kiss – then leaves our daughter in my care. I have no idea what to do with her today, but I don't even get time to think about it before Abby comes in with a deep frown, her face all creased up like something is bothering her.

I swear, nobody can balance their moods in this house.

'Something on your mind, sis?'

'Not really. I'm just bored and wondered if you want to do something today.'

'Things have changed slightly. I've got Mia.'

Abby smiles thinly at Mia, then looks out the window. 'Couldn't she come with us?'

'Come with us where, exactly?'

'I thought maybe you could show me around town.'

It's not like I'd be doing anything wrong, but I know Louise is feeling pretty sensitive as of late. Taking her baby out of the house might not be the best idea, but it would also feel wrong to not live our lives like normal people. Mia is only a year old, but she still deserves to get out and enjoy her first full summer. Is that too selfish?

'Fine, if we can make it quick.'

'Okay, but let's have lunch as well.' Abby smiles widely. 'My treat.'

'Right, with whose money?'

'Yours, of course.'

We both laugh while I take Mia and change her into something more summery. I really do intend to send Louise a text and let her know, but in all the chaos of parenting while leading a village tour, it slips from my mind as quickly as it entered.

I'll have to deal with the consequences later.

Mia is in a beautiful yellow dress that brings out the brightness of her eyes. She's smiling in the Jaguar's back seat as I get her out, sweetly mistaking walk time for playtime. I smile back because the combination of the blue summer sky and being surrounded by loved ones brings me the kind of joy I haven't had in years.

Maybe even pre-Louise.

I'm wearing shorts, despite hating it, because the sun is too blisteringly hot. Abby is also wearing a long dress that reaches her knees, her figure a little slimmer than how she normally likes it. It's probably because of the prison food, but I try not to think about it because then I might slip up and say something. I don't want to remind her of the horrific crash years ago, where one simple misjudgement of a bend in the road cost someone their life.

Nobody ever talks about what it cost *us*, however. As it should, a wealth of sympathy went towards the family of the young lady who died, but Abby was cast as a villain through no fault of her own. The judge took no leniency on her because she'd been driving for five years at that point and said she should have known better. So off to prison she went for six long years, leaving me behind without even letting me see her due to some stupid vanity problem. I could've told her I didn't care what she looked like, but she might not have listened anyway.

So I make sure to tell her now.

'You look lovely,' I say, and she turns with a big, smug grin. 'Radiant, even.'

'Shut up.' She laughs and moves to hit me, then spots Mia in my arms and stops.

We walk around Dolcester, high on life and over the moon to be reunited. While the sun is out and the kids run past us with their water guns, it's easy to forget the way Louise has been acting. My mind is barely on it at all, I'm so focused on showing Abby the docks where the pirates had a battle with the British in the seventeenth century. We walk through the luscious green park, where picnickers and dog walkers all say hello, as is the custom for village life in England. Mia waves at everyone, of course, because she loves people as much as I do.

As much as I love *her*.

Lunchtime comes around, and we find a bench in the garden of my favourite pub. It overlooks a river – it's technically a canal, but you would never guess it – where some familiar faces beam while they paddle their canoes. Abby orders us both beers and some burgers with chips. Normally I'd serve packed food to Mia, but she's fallen asleep in her buggy. It must be nice to get some rest. Especially in the shade, where the sun can't get to her.

While we wait for our food, I sip on the cold, refreshing beer and gaze over at Abby. She's gazing back with that look of suspicion, probably wondering if something is up. A flutter of excitement flies through me, and words can't describe how happy I am to see my sister again. I hope nothing ever comes between us.

Especially not Louise.

'Can you stop staring at me?' she says jokingly. 'It's getting weird.'

'Sorry, I'm just so glad you're out. Have you thought about what to do next?'

'You mean where to live?'

'Not that I'm kicking you out – you're welcome to stay as long as you like – but you might need a plan about where to look for a job. Maybe you need some money to help get you started? When you're ready, that is. In the meantime, I'd rather you stick around.'

Abby smiles, and the food comes out. I reach for my burger, but she doesn't touch hers because now it's her turn to stare. It makes me conscious, so I linger with the burger near my mouth, meeting her eyes, which are starting to cloud over.

'What's wrong?' I ask.

'It's just... I really appreciate what you're doing for me. The house, welcoming me into your family, letting me spend so much time with your little ray of sunshine. I just want you to know how grateful I am that, of all the people in the world, God chose you to be my brother.'

'Are you getting religious now? Did prison do this to you?'

'Shut up,' she says and laughs again. 'God, fate, destiny. Call it whatever you want. The fact remains I'm fortunate to have you. And you're doing so well! What with your successful career and that amazing house. And your wife—'

'Stop.' I hold up my hand.

'What?'

'You don't have to pretend you like her.'

'Who? Louise?'

'Yes. You hate each other, so let's just not act otherwise.'

Abby nods, the smile fading from her face as she grabs a chip and drags it through a puddle of ketchup. 'Whatever you say, Doc. But for the record, I don't hate her. I just wish she would be a bit nicer to me. She has no reason to behave any other way.'

'She seems to think you do.'

'Well, she's a relatively new mum. Maybe it's hormones or having someone on her home turf or something. However all this turns out, I'm still going to try my best to get on with her.'

I don't say anything else, but I believe her. Abby has always been great with people, even if that's not reflecting in her relationship with Louise. But I'm not about to let the thought of my wife's strange behaviour ruin an otherwise perfect day. So I just sit here and eat my burger, enjoying the thick, juicy meat with the best woman I know right in front of me. I only stop to raise my glass for a toast.

'Here's to long-overdue reunions.'

'And for the importance of family.'

Abby clinks her beer against mine, and then we continue to eat in silence.

WE DON'T SPEAK of Louise for the rest of the day, but she does cross my mind a couple of times. Mainly because I'm worried I might have to follow through on a certain threat. Just in case it's unclear, I love my wife to the stars and back again, but if she can't find a way to get along with my sister, then it's hard to see a future with her in it. What would that mean for Mia?

I have no idea.

We finish our tour of the town, bumping into some locals who ask me – as they always do – if I can fit them in for some urgent appointments. It's hard to tell them no, but I can't favour one person over the other, so I kindly explain they'll have to take it up with Ethel. My own mind is busy enough with all my domestic drama.

Although I keep that to myself.

Those same people introduce themselves to Abby, who reminds me of a princess in her gracious way. She's smiling and asking about the other people, and I can tell everyone likes her. It takes me back to when I first came to the village and everyone was just as kind and welcoming to me, but Louise – who showed me around town before I eventually asked her to marry me – seemed to never quite be one with the people. Like she was an outsider. There's no judgement from me, but it's interesting to compare that woman to the person she is now.

She still hasn't learned how to communicate well.

After a long and tiring walk in the sun, we make it back to the Jaguar. It's like an oven, so Abby plays with Mia outside while I run the air con to cool down the car. When it's finally time to go home, it hits me that I didn't end up sending a text message to Louise.

She must be worried sick.

Time soon proves that to be the case because

she's standing on the driveway when we pull up, hunched over in the shade with her arms around her stomach. Before I even kill the engine, she's tearing open the rear door and pulling Mia out of the seat. I try to stop her, telling her to calm down while trying to squeeze in an apology, but she just shoots me an infuriated glare before pointing at Abby and starting to snarl.

'What made you think I wanted you to take my daughter out all day with *her*?'

Louise slams the door. Mia starts to wail. All the while, I'm left alone in the car with Abby, embarrassed and uncomfortable. It upsets me that she had to hear that, but it also lends to my theory that Louise is slowly starting to lose control.

I'm really starting to worry about her.

Not to mention our marriage.

Chapter 12
Louise

Mia still hasn't stopped screaming by the time we reach the house. I'm not sure if it's the shouting or the slamming of the car door that upset her. It might just be that she felt the same anger as me, which only got worse when Daniel looked at me like I was a crazy person.

Okay, so I know that could've been handled better, but what am I supposed to think? He was the one who insisted I went upstairs for a nap. The next thing I know, he's out of the house for a few hours with that perfect little sister of his, without so much as a text to let me know where he went. I even tried calling him many times, but there was no answer.

This one is on him.

The Sister-in-Law

Mia's screaming dials up to eleven. Her face is beetroot red, and now she's getting herself all worked up. I don't bother waiting for Daniel, who's taking the time to park his precious car in the garage. Instead, I take Mia upstairs and give her a snack in the nursery. She soothes almost instantly while I relax in the rocking chair. I know this feeling of hers.

She's tired.

It feels like my heart will never stop racing. My mind is a busy roundabout of the same old thoughts: why is Abby like she is, why does Daniel trust her so much, and why is he always taking her word over mine? It's unsettling, and I think Mia is picking up on my ever-increasing heart rate, so I try to mellow out with some comforting thoughts.

For instance, the cameras I had installed while they were out.

It began with a phone call to an old flame. George runs a small shop out of his living room on the other end of the village. Although he sells most of his parts online and ships out large quantities every day, he does perform the occasional task for the locals. It's more of a courtesy than anything – his way of giving back to the village that raised him. My feelings for him – and definitely my lust – are non-existent now, and he knows as much.

But that didn't mean he wouldn't come to the house as an emergency.

The cameras are a little bulky but should go unnoticed. George assured me people rarely found them and that I should trust him. So I did. An hour later, we had three cameras set up: one in the nursery to cover blind spots that the monitor can't reach, one in the kitchen, and another in the living room. I thought about setting one up in Abby's room, but I knew that was crossing a line.

The thought does make me happy. I'm safeguarded now, finally able to talk to Abby however I like because it will actually help me if she lashes out. At least then, I can show it to Daniel and prove once and for all that his sister is a psycho.

My heart settles. I'm calm, and now Mia is, too. Her eyes start closing, so I slowly transfer her to the cot and watch her for a while. My precious little girl, who I love so much that it makes me sick. When I think about Abby taking her into her arms, a cold shiver runs through me. How am I supposed to compete with Miss Perfect?

It's simple: I just sit back and wait.

. . .

When I'm certain she's down to sleep, I head downstairs, feeling an obvious discomfort in the room. Abby is sitting on the sofa and flicking through one of my magazines without so much as looking up. Daniel is standing in the kitchen doorway, leaning against the frame with his arms folded. I can tell he's cooking something because the smell is wafting through.

He shoots me a look that says he wants to talk, so I follow him into the kitchen.

The smell is stronger here. I take a look in the saucepan on the hob and see he has a bolognese on the go. My favourite meal, which can only mean it's apology food. I turn to him, ready to ask about it, but he's already talking before I can get a word out.

'I just want to say sorry for earlier.' Daniel leans against the worktop. 'I should have let you know where we were going. I really did mean to text you, but I just got distracted looking after both Mia and Abby. If it's any consolation, it wasn't planned.'

'It wasn't?'

'No. I intended to stay at home. Abby was the one who asked for a village tour.'

Of course she was. Daniel wouldn't make such

a careless decision if it weren't for a good reason, and it seems he'd do absolutely anything for his sister. Does that make me feel inferior – as though I'm suddenly the least important person in the house? Hell yes, as the kids say. But I know from experience that talking about it only makes things worse.

'Apology accepted,' I tell him.

The rest of the day is surprisingly calm. We all hang out together downstairs, including Mia when she wakes up from her nap. As the afternoon rolls into evening and she gets a little sleepy again, I sit there and cuddle her while we watch a family film about some talking dogs. I don't know the name of it because I don't really care.

I'm too focused on keeping my baby out of Abby's arms.

There is one problem ticking along in the background, however. The others don't know, but I'm fully aware there's a camera on us. I'll review the footage later on with the mobile app, but for now, it almost feels like I'm performing. Just like Abby does when Daniel is around. It feels stilted and unnatural. Is this how she feels all the time? Like she's betraying her own self?

Later tonight, when everyone is in bed, I go to the bathroom and take my phone with me. Sitting on the edge of the bath with a tired fuzz humming in my ears, I open the app and study all of the footage. To save time, I gloss over all of the scenes with me in them – I know what happened when I was there – and go straight for everyone's more private moments.

I don't like what I find.

First of all, there's Daniel. He's taking time out in the kitchen, leaning back against the worktop as he often does when he's stressed. The timer says it was just after six, and I remember that moment very well. Abby and I were stuck in a room together, and she didn't so much as glance at me. It was like she knew I could catch her out and refused to act. But Daniel just runs his hands through his dark hair, huffing out a breath like he's stressed.

I actually sort of feel for him. Despite feeling slightly annoyed that he's always siding with his sister, I do understand the situation he's in. Two people he loves dearly are at each other's throats – one more literally than the other – and he's right in the middle of it. His feelings are on my mind every time something big happens, but I really don't want Abby to win this. I don't want Abby to tear apart my family.

I'm suddenly awake when Daniel looks up at the camera. My blood is pulsing through my body, my heart hammering against my chest as he comes away from the worktop and studies the camera. I realise I'm caught and that things are about to get a lot worse. He's squinting like he knows I'm watching, somehow frowning at the same time. He reaches out a hand, and I start to sweat. His hand closes as he grabs for the camera, and I know it's all over.

But then he walks away.

Confused, I replay those moments again and see nothing different until I let time go by. Daniel has his hands cupped, walking slowly towards the back door as he manages to open it with his elbow, then throws a spider into the garden.

I breathe a long sigh of relief and review the rest of the footage. There's nothing there. Nothing helpful, anyway. But there will be other days in which I can find hard evidence of Abby being every bit as nasty as I know she is.

All I have to do is wait.

· · ·

My good luck comes just two days later. At least I think it does.

Abby has spent the day sneaking in evil smirks whenever Daniel has his back turned. Just as she's always done, she waits until her brother is in the room before asking to hold Mia. I know what she's doing – she *wants* me to say no. She *wants* Daniel to see how I'm not making an effort to trust her. I'm not going to give her the satisfaction.

Mia goes to her too easily now, squealing with excitement as her fun Aunt Abby takes her into her loving arms. Daniel gives me a look as if to tell me he told me so, but I don't respond to it. Our marriage is already rocky, and I don't want to push it over the edge.

In other words, I'm not going to fall for her tricks.

Abby knows it, too, because she's advanced to grinning at me even when Daniel is in the same room. This morning, she actually went as far as nudging me while I was holding a hot cup of coffee. I kept this to myself, of course, telling Daniel I accidentally hit the banister with my elbow. He asked if I was okay. Abby told me not to be clumsy.

But I'm watching.

Every time she behaves a certain way, it always happens to be far away from the cameras. I'm trying my best to stay near them so if she does anything, there will be concrete proof of exactly what she's like. Somehow, she manages to avoid it.

Until today.

I put Mia to bed an hour ago. Daniel, Abby, and I are all sitting in the living room, rewatching the early seasons of a crime drama so Abby can catch up. I hate that she won't do it in her own time, seeing as she still doesn't have a job or anything even closely resembling a hobby. Now I have to suffer the slow start to a series I never truly loved in the first place.

Mia starts crying, unsettled in her cot. I get up to go, but Abby shoots to her feet and insists that she should be the one to help her. I tell her no, but Daniel gives me that look again. Normally I would fight against it, but tonight, I want to see every one of her private moments.

Even if she is alone with my child.

When Abby leaves the room, I excuse myself and go to the downstairs bathroom. Daniel barely looks up from the TV, and I wonder if he'll even notice I'm gone. When I lock myself away, I sit on the toilet lid and open the app, watching every little move my sister-in-law makes.

Not much happens at first. She's already taken Mia into her arms and walks around the room, shushing her. Mia's beautiful little eyes are halfway to closing, twisting the knife in my heart because Abby seems to have that magic touch. I'm feeling rancid little pangs of jealousy because it always takes me twice as long, even though I'm her mother.

Once again, Abby has the better of me.

There's nothing to report. In fact, she's a little *too* good. She passes back and forth as she paces the room until Mia is sound asleep in her arms. Then she moves to the cot, lowering her in and standing there to admire her as if it's her own daughter. I'm trying not to hate her, but she's making it as difficult as possible. If not just from being a sly little witch, then from being the perfect auntie whenever Daniel is around to see it.

But not tonight.

Tonight, she turns around and faces the camera. I freeze, wondering if she might have seen it, but then I remember how George said it's practically invisible to the naked eye – that you'd have to be looking really hard if you wanted to find it. Maybe Abby *did* look.

Because she winks right at me, then leaves the room.

No wonder she's behaving herself.

She knows she's being watched.

Chapter 13
Daniel

As TIME GOES BY, things are starting to improve. There hasn't been an incident between Abby and Louise in days. I hope this is the start of something new – a sort of silent agreement that they'll be civil towards one another, even if they don't truly like each other.

It's not ideal though, I think as I pack up work for the day. The truth is, I'm a little apprehensive about going home tonight. I wish I could stay here at the office just to be far away from the blast radius, but putting in overtime also forces those two to be in the house together. I've heard somebody call that exposure therapy, which seems apt.

I finish packing, my computer shut down and my desk cleared when there's a knock on the door.

When I shout for them to enter, Ethel opens the door and pokes her head through the crack, her large glasses brushing the frame. She looks too serious for my liking.

'What is it?' I ask.

'A gentleman has called for an urgent appointment.'

'Can't it wait until tomorrow?'

'Okay, I can tell him to—'

'Actually, hold on.' I pause for a moment to gather my thoughts. Although it's true that I have to head back eventually, perhaps it wouldn't be the worst idea to help out one last villager before heading back. 'Send him in.'

I won't disclose the details of the patient's problem, but I will tell you I make a mountain out of a molehill, turning my computer back on and asking far more questions than I should. The patient has absolutely nothing to worry about, but I still find myself killing time by investigating it, even though I figured out it's benign a while back. This whole charade actually makes me feel severely guilty. Why can't I just go home like a normal person?

When I've finally run out of excuses, I return to the house and enter the garage. I try to focus on

Mia, who is the best part of any day. Using this to encourage myself, I'm quickly very warmed and excited by the idea of holding my baby girl in my arms again. That's enough to make me leave the garage and go into the house.

That's when I know things have got worse.

Abby is sitting on the stairs in the main hall, her elbows resting on her lap while her hands cup her cheeks. She gives a half-smile that's about as genuine as a politician. There's no way she can hide that glum expression from me, no matter how hard she tries.

'What's wrong now?' I ask, dreading the answer.

'It's nothing.'

'We both know that's not true. Out with it.'

Abby sits up straight and pulls the kind of chewing face she normally does when making a big decision. When she looks up from the floor and her gaze meets mine, it's easy to see the sparkle of residual tears in her eyes. I go to her, calm on the outside but panicking on the inside.

'Hey, tell me what's wrong,' I say, cupping her hand.

It takes a while for her to come around, but when she does, the one word that leaves her lips is enough to ruin my day. Perhaps more than that – it could be that this has derailed my entire week, month, or even life. Because I'm so sick of hearing it that I could scream.

'Louise,' she says.

And it only gets worse from there.

The tears come again, streaming down her cheeks like twin rivers that drop into her lap. I hold her hand, just like I always used to. I want her to know that I'm here for her, no matter how hard things get. No matter who stands in our way.

But of course it's Louise. I've been trying so hard to accept the possibility that their entire rivalry has just been figments of their imaginations. Abby has never been one for lying, but I sort of hoped some of the things my wife has done were slight exaggerations. It's the only way I can come to terms with all that's happened, and to be totally honest, it's starting to look like there's no end to this awful madness.

'Tell me what happened,' I say.

Abby shakes her head, looks around, then points to the corners of the room. I don't understand fully, even when I try to look. It occurs to me then that I haven't heard a peep from Louise or

Mia. I've been so preoccupied with my sister that I forgot all about them.

'Where are they?' I ask.

'Upstairs somewhere, watching.'

'Watching? What does that mean?'

'I can't say. Not here.'

My heart won't stop fluttering. Anxiety builds up inside me, provoking me to ask the big question but dreading the answer. I shove my briefcase to one side and lean in close to Abby's ear, ready to hear it. 'Do we need to go into the living room?'

'No, not there,' she says hurriedly, as if frightened of something.

'Where, then?'

'The back room.'

Abby gets up and leads the way, wrapping her arms around herself. She looks like the victim of an assault, stumbling home and feeling ashamed of what's just happened. I can hear her sniffles, and my heart is breaking all over again. She's had such a tough life that I just want things to get better for her. She deserves that much, at the very least.

We reach the back room, and she stands in the doorway with the lights off. Something is seriously wrong, but I can't imagine how bad things must be for her to act this strangely. For a moment, I wonder if Louise might have been right – that the woman who came out of prison is not the same woman that went in. I hear people change on the inside. Is that what this is?

My suspicions end there, however, when Abby tells me what the problem is.

'There are cameras,' she says. 'Set up around the house to spy on me.'

I freeze, unable to find the right words. Is she paranoid? Is this some kind of mental delusion – an unfortunate side effect of the tragedy that occurred in the car all those years ago? I start picturing a new future, one where she's getting professional help and Louise... I don't know where she is. Or Mia, for that matter.

'What makes you think that?' I ask, fearful of her response.

'I've seen them. There's one in the kitchen, one in the living room, and another in the nursery. There might be more, but those are the ones I've found.'

'There's already a camera in the nursery.'

'Well, now there's another one on the other side of the room.'

'Okay, and who put the cameras there?'

'Who do you think?'

I must admit I don't have much trouble believing her. Louise has been acting far too bizarrely of late, and this would explain why Abby looks as scared as she does. And although I want to believe it's not true – that Louise wouldn't go this far – I have to at least give Abby the chance to prove that it's true. That Louise is now spying on my family.

'Show me.'

I MUST CONFESS I don't truly believe it until I see the cameras. Abby points to them all one by one, and I feel stupid for so many reasons: I trusted Louise to make more of an effort, I've been spied on in my own house, and I didn't even see the cameras. It makes me wonder just how long they've been here – how long my personal time hasn't been so personal.

'Is that all of them?' I ask as Abby hands me the third camera. Louise is still upstairs, and I wonder if she's been watching any of this. She's in for a shock if she thinks I'm going to be okay with what she's done. I'm absolutely fuming.

'It's all I can find,' Abby says. 'I hope there aren't more.'

'I'll take care of it. Why don't you spend the rest of the evening in the guest bedroom?'

Abby seems to recognise the look on my face – if it at all resembles how I'm feeling, she knows I'm about to seriously lose it. She nods, pours herself a large glass of water, then leaves the kitchen. I'm all alone with my thoughts. There's nothing to do but wait.

I still can't believe she's gone this far.

It takes half an hour for Louise to come back downstairs. I assume she's about to start cooking for the family, but my appetite went a long time ago. As soon as she enters the room with that innocent smile of hers, I feel stupid for ever having fallen for it.

It's quickly replaced by a frown.

'What's wrong?' she asks, Mia pointing giddily in her arms.

'Is there something you want to tell me?'

'Not that I can think of...'

If it wasn't bad enough that she's been spying on us, I'm heartbroken to discover she won't confess to it even when given the chance. I want Louise to redeem herself, so I give her one last chance, spelling it out for her in absolute terms.

'Have you been spying on us?' I ask bluntly, watching her reaction from across the room.

She barely changes, her face still a picture of dumb confusion. It makes me hate her, honestly. Not just for this incident alone but for all the unnecessary crap leading up to it. Who exactly does she think she is?

'What do you mean?' she asks. 'Of course I've not been spying on you.'

'Are you sure?'

'Positive.'

I sigh, greatly disappointed that she's still lying to me, then point to the cameras sitting on the worktop on the other side of the kitchen. She follows the direction of my finger, sees the mess of devices and wires, then slowly nods acceptance as she puts Mia in her high chair. She then sits across from me, as if we're two business people having a formal conversation.

'This is the situation you put me in,' she says. 'By not trusting me.'

'You're blaming this on me?' My heart thumps heavily as anger courses through my veins like molten lava. 'After everything you've done to my sister, you're actually blaming this on me? Just when I thought you couldn't get any worse...'

'It's not like that. I needed you to see.'

'To see what? That you've lost all control of your senses?'

'No. Abby is—'

'Abby is a sweet woman who doesn't deserve any of the grief you're giving her.'

'You're wrong!' Louise shouts loud enough for Mia to start crying.

I lean over and stroke her hair, which always calms her, but my eyes don't leave Louise's. 'All I ever asked from you was that you make my sister feel welcome in this house. Since the very beginning, I've heard nothing but accusations and bullying.'

'*She's* the bully.'

'Don't. Just... don't.' I hold my hand up to halt the conversation, putting every ounce of effort into remaining calm. I can barely look at her any more because everything she says and does only fuels my rage. It's all I can do to keep it together. For Mia's sake. 'Just tell me if there are any more cameras we need to worry about.'

Louise takes a while to answer. It's unclear what she's thinking, but the little huff of surrender makes me think she's telling the truth. 'No, there were only three of them.'

'How long were they there, Louise?'

'Days. Hardly.'

I feel sick, violated, and – most of all – disappointed. Until now, I thought I married the most perfect woman in the world. It turns out she's as bad as the small flings who came before her, putting her insane theories before her own family. But I'm not a monster. I know when someone needs help, and I did vow to be there for her, in sickness and in health.

'I'd like you to see a professional,' I say calmly.

'I don't need to—'

'See a professional, or we're finished.'

That's all I have to say. I get up from my chair and leave the kitchen, but I only make it to the door before one last thing pops into my head – something I feel compelled to say because it perfectly sums up how I've been feeling.

'I'm starting to hate you,' I tell her.

Finally, I leave the room, feeling disgusted and ashamed.

Chapter 14
The Watcher

She steps off the coach and stands in the dust as it departs without her. There's one bag in her hand, which is full of only the most vital things: something to eat, something to wear, and, most importantly of all, something to drink.

There's a mission for her in the small village of Dolcester, which she intends to complete regardless of the outcome. The Watcher begins to walk, following the directions on her printed sheet of paper that tells her where to go. It's only a ten-minute walk, but that's harder than it sounds in the furnace-like heat of July. Especially when her hangover intensifies.

She finds herself at the bed and breakfast,

checking in and lying about her reasons for visiting the quaint little village. She's here to write an article, she says, and that's about the sum total of her excuse. It's not like she can tell the truth, is it?

That she's here to save a life.

The room is small, dark, and depressing, but it offers a bed – a place to lie down and fidget as she tries to sleep, but countless cruel dreams haunt her one after the other. She doesn't want to be here, but she has to be. She needs to see for herself that Abby Wright is walking free and, if need be, to interfere with the process.

Because it can't happen again.

The Watcher is all alone now. Not just in the room but in life. She'll never get back what was taken from her, but if she can stop it from happening to someone else, then maybe she can find a way to be happy – to sleep at night knowing it doesn't have to end in suicide. That she's done something right for once in her pitiful life, and she deserves a rest.

It starts with a simple social media message, but it's more than that. Once you take a closer look and understand the true reason behind it, you begin to uncover layers you didn't know were there. That's why she came to this village in the first place. Not just to reach out to someone but to send a warning.

And maybe – just maybe – save a life.

Chapter 15
Louise

IT'S BEEN a few days since Daniel told me to see a professional, and I booked an appointment with a sweet lady in town named Priscilla. We're due a consultation two weeks from now, which I have no intention of attending. What it means is that I have a very limited time in which to prove Abby is a liar and to find out why she's been acting like this towards me.

It feels like a betrayal that Daniel is always siding with her, but I know how it looks. Abby is always the first one to tell her side of the story, so one would naturally believe it. It doesn't help that I hid those cameras – what a waste of time that was – and proved he couldn't trust me. No wonder he wants me to seek help.

I'm starting to feel a little crazy myself.

But there's no time to think about it today. Today is Daniel's birthday, and despite him choosing his allegiance with Abby, he's still my husband, and I'll treat him as such. I picked his main gift up from the market the day after Abby arrived, and I'm going to bake a cake from scratch while Daniel spends time with Mia and his sister.

This is the first time I've baked in years. I used to do it all the time, enjoying finding the perfect recipe and taking time to decorate it, pouring all my effort and skill into the tiny little details. Most people would just opt for a simple message on top, but I like to make flowers and vines of the icing around the edge. That's what I want to make for my husband today.

Not just a cake.

A gesture.

The base is good to go. I slide it into the oven and set the heat, then head into the living room. There's no sign of Abby, which takes a massive weight off my shoulders, so I sit with Daniel and try to spend a little quality time with him, playing with Mia between my legs.

'Is there anything in particular you want to do today?' I ask.

'Not really. You know I hate birthdays.'

'We both know that's not true. You might hate getting older, but I know for a fact you enjoy the celebration. How about we all go out for dinner tonight?'

'Is it practical now that we have Mia?'

'We went last year, didn't we?'

'She was a lot less work then.'

I shrug. 'If you don't want to go, that's fine.'

Daniel pulls a face like he's thinking, then lifts his gaze to look at me. I must have the worst poker face in the world because he brightens up like he used to do when it was just the two of us. Before Abby entered our world and turned it upside down.

'You already booked it, didn't you?'

'Sorry,' I say, laughing. 'It's at Denzil's.'

'Really? You booked that for me?'

I nod, enjoying his reaction. Denzil's is his favourite restaurant. There aren't a whole lot of options for eating out in Dolcester, basically leaving us with two smaller, cheaper restaurants or this fancy one that's very hard to get a seat in. He seems to like the surprise, as evidenced by his widening grin, then leans forward to kiss me. I welcome it because it's been so long.

'The reservation is at seven,' I tell him.

'What reservation?' Abby's voice sounds from behind me, and it feels like a dark cloud has drawn overhead, dampening my mood with a dreary aura. She looks from me to Daniel, as if he should be the one to answer, then asks again, 'What reservation?'

'Louise is taking us out tonight.'

'Really?' She looks at me, smiling. 'I'm allowed to come?'

'Of course you are,' I say. 'You're family.'

Forcing those words out is enough to make me feel sick. I really didn't want her to come, but if she can keep up appearances, then so can I. It's just two more weeks, I remind myself. Surely I can bite my tongue for that short while. Or until I find proof that she's scum.

Whichever comes first.

Abby comes to sit with us, but she doesn't make it that far. We're interrupted by a high-pitched, rapid beeping that pierces the air with alarming urgency. Mia starts crying as we all cover our ears, but it takes a second to register what's happened.

The smoke detector has been set off.

Because I left the cake unattended.

. . .

The kitchen is engulfed in thick plumes of black smoke. Daniel rushes past me and runs for the window, shoving it open while I swipe a towel off the side and start fanning. Abby hangs back, watching the show with little Mia kneeling at her side. At least they're away from the smoke.

Even if Abby was the one who caused it.

It begins to clear, giving me a second to open the oven and refill the room with the toxic smog. It billows out in a puff of black, my oven glove getting singed as I pull the cake out and dump it into the sink. I let the tap run cold, then stand there both angry and disheartened that all my effort has amounted to nothing more than a solid, black rock.

'It's okay,' Daniel says, patting me on the shoulder. 'You tried.'

Yes, I did try, and I don't believe for a second that I accidentally turned up the heat. I think back to only minutes ago, when Abby appeared from nowhere. She must have taken a detour through the kitchen, tampering with the oven before coming in and acting all innocent. I'm starting to crumble, my life falling apart at the hands of this ungrateful, nasty young woman who is out to get me, and the worst part is I don't even know why.

'This wasn't...' I'm about to tell Daniel my theory, but I remember I must act naturally. He can't know about my disdain for Abby because I need to keep him around until she's proven guilty of everything she's done. So all I can do for now is shake my head.

I don't even get to finish my sentence.

Daniel leaves the room and takes Mia. She's staring into the kitchen with her mouth agape, mesmerised by her first-ever glimpse of a cooking disaster. But that doesn't stop her dad from being playful, nuzzling into her cheek and making her giggle.

'Thanks for trying,' he says on his way out. 'We still have dinner to look forward to.'

When he's gone, I'm left alone with Abby. She's staring me down like I've done something to wrong her, and I guess I have – setting up those cameras almost got her caught. Now that they're disposed of, she's free to act however she damn well pleases.

She seizes advantage of that immediately.

'Phew,' she says, stepping into the kitchen and looking down at the mess in the sink. 'You almost succeeded in doing something nice for my brother then. It's a shame you put it in at the wrong heat, otherwise it could have been delicious.'

'Cut the crap,' I snap at her, making her smile maniacally. 'I've never burned a cake in my life. This was you, changing the heat when we had our backs turned.'

'Now now. There's no proof of that.'

'There doesn't need to be. I know the truth.'

'Hmm. It's a shame nobody would agree with you.'

As soon as the words leave her lips, she takes one step closer to me. I hold my breath, wondering what she's about to do as she leans towards my ear, her voice a harsh, cutting whisper that shakes me to my core.

'That's your punishment for spying on me,' she says. 'Don't test me again.'

As if nothing happened, she steps away with a big, friendly smile and walks away. I stand there, afraid and amazed at how quickly she went from demon witch to sweet sister, practically skipping into the next room to spend some time with my husband.

I guess this is my mess to clean up.

And I don't just mean the burned cake.

. . .

DENZIL'S IS A DIMLY LIT, romantic restaurant that only opens three days per week. They overcharge on everything, but it's true that you get what you pay for, so it's not *really* overpaying. Besides, this meal is on me, straight from my savings that I worked years for.

That's why it irks me that Abby has come along.

We arrive at seven on the dot. Daniel has suggested Abby stays with Mia for the duration so he and I can enjoy our dinner in peace for once. It's not the worst idea, especially as they'll still be sitting at our table where I can keep an eye on my baby, but I still hate that he's pushing for his nightmare of a sister to take an important role in our special night. Then again, it's his birthday, so who am I to argue?

After all, I'm still playing along just to keep him happy.

The dinner itself goes surprisingly well. There's not a single interruption, save a social media message from a stranger that I'll read later. It's peaceful and elegant here. We've all ordered big off the menu, even Abby, who grabbed the most expensive steak there was, then left most of it untouched. But worse things have happened. I'm just glad we could enjoy some food and a bottle of wine without any drama exploding in my face.

But I speak too soon.

I start to panic when I go into the bottom of Mia's buggy for Daniel's main gift. It's a first edition of *The Magic Finger*, signed by Roald Dahl himself. It was his favourite book growing up, and I know he treasures things like this. I managed to snag it at the bargain price of £1600, which seems a lot for a book, but it's worth a lot more. I had to hunt for it, too, eventually arranging it from a seller at the market. I picked it up that day we went in with Abby, but now it's nowhere to be seen.

'What's wrong?' Daniel asks as I more desperately search the buggy.

'Your present. I had it here for you.'

'Oh, don't worry about it. You've done enough for me already.'

I know I have, but that's not the point. It cost an absolute fortune and would mean the world to him, so I'm starting to sweat at the thought of losing it. Although I barely manage to continue my search before it presents itself.

In Abby's hands.

'Well, maybe while you look for it, I can give him *my* gift.'

I'm sitting here amazed, my mouth hanging open with absolute disbelief as she hands it over to Daniel. He studies it curiously, telling her she didn't need to do this, and she really didn't. It's the same size and shape as the book I got for him. It's in the same wrapping paper that I keep at the back of my own wardrobe. And judging by the look on his face when he creates a small tear in the packaging, it's the very same book I purchased.

'My God, Abby. How on earth did you manage to get this?' he says.

'I called in a favour from an old friend.'

'But it must have cost an arm and a leg!'

'It's nothing compared to what you've done for me.'

I excuse myself and leave the table while he gives her a kiss on the cheek and sets the record for the world's longest hug. I head outside for some air, taking my phone with me to read the message. But I can't concentrate.

How dare she steal my gift, much less hand it to him in front of me and pretend it was from her? She must know I'm unable to complain about her – she's been setting it up that way for a while now –

and she's right: she does own me, and there's nothing I can do about it.

But that's about to change because the stranger on my phone has information.

And I can't wait to use it against her.

Chapter 16
Daniel

I'm working from home today, just so I can keep an eye on them.

It's no secret they don't get on, and yesterday was just too good to be true. I thought birthdays were supposed to be nice events, surrounded by loved ones and merriment and all the good stuff. But I can read Louise like a book, and she just wasn't having any fun.

Speaking of books, something isn't right about my copy of *The Magic Finger*. I could have sworn I saw Louise tuck away a gift of similar shape and size at the market. But her gift for me went missing and still hasn't turned up. Worse yet, Abby pulled a stunt like that out of nowhere. I wonder for a second if she might have stolen it and passed it off as her own gift.

Then I shake it off. That's a ridiculous way of thinking – Louise would have surely said something if that was the case. Then again, maybe not, because I know she's putting in a lot of effort to make things work between the three of us. All I can really do is accept the gift and be grateful for spending time with my family – those two and my perfect little baby girl.

But today is wildly different from yesterday. It's all work, slaving away at my desk in the spare room and catching up on some things. I have cases to close, people to check up on via telephone, and a virtual meeting with a man from Leeds who wants to come and learn under me on an internship as he's in his first year as a medical student. It's a big ask, I know, which is exactly what I'll tell him. Along with the fact I just don't have the time.

By three o'clock, I'm completely out of energy. Most of my catch-up work is done, but – as is often the case – more tasks have built up to take their place. I'm starting to wonder if I can stick it out in such a limited practice. I honestly thought it would be easier, with the village being so small. Why does everyone become ill at the same time?

It's time for a break. I can't keep plugging away at this while exhaustion tugs at my eyelids. I need to lie down, even if only for a minute, so I open my door to listen out for trouble downstairs – right where Louise and Abby are hanging out with my daughter – and hear nothing, then retreat to the sofa we put in the office for such times.

I want to sleep. *Need* to. But the tension from yesterday's dinner keeps popping up in my mind. It elevates my heart rate, stirs some otherwise dormant anxiety that keeps me awake. Ten minutes pass by too quickly, and I'm still wired, staring at the ceiling and wondering how things got this bad. Having Abby here was supposed to be the start of her new life and a chance to reconnect after all these years.

It's not supposed to end in divorce.

After a lot of meditation and self-talk, my eyes finally start to close. My body is relaxing, and I can feel my worries melt away. It's only temporary, but that's all I need. Just enough to slip into a half-hour nap to recharge, and then my entire outlook will take better shape. I'm slipping, a wave of fatigue burying me as I start to snooze in the peaceful room, away from it all.

Then comes the knock. Three hard taps against the door. I must admit, I'm angry to have been disturbed because there's a sign on the door warning that I shouldn't be. But I'm not about to take it out on whoever is there because the mood in this house is already at an all-time low, so I just call for them to enter.

The door opens slightly, and Abby's head appears in the small gap. She's not smiling, unlike her usual self, which makes me worry about what might have happened now.

'Can we talk?' she asks.

I sigh, sit up, and pat the sofa next to me.

It's no wonder my stress levels are so high.

The concern on her wrinkled-up face is instantly noticeable, but I let her come and sit beside me and speak when she's ready. It doesn't take long because she crosses her legs and wraps her arms around herself, her head hanging low as she starts to explain.

'I think I should leave,' she says.

My mouth opens, but no words come out because I simply don't know what to say. Abby notices this and then nods slowly as she begins to elaborate. 'Ever since I got here, there's been nothing but trouble. I've been blaming Louise the whole time, and she's been blaming me. You two seem happy, and I don't want to get in the way of that, so maybe I should move on.'

'You'll do no such thing,' I tell her, putting a hand gently on her arm. 'You're my sister – you're *family* – and you'll always be welcome here. Just because things are a little uncomfortable at the moment, it doesn't mean they won't improve. Louise is seeing a professional soon, and... I don't know. She's trying, isn't she?'

'No, she is, but there's still tension between us.'

'There's bound to be. For a little while, anyway.'

'That's just it. I don't have a little while.'

'What's that supposed to mean?'

Abby shakes her head, as if telling herself she shouldn't say what's on her mind. I lightly shake the arm I have my hand on, dropping my serious tone as I tell her she can speak – that there are no cameras. Thankfully, she smiles a little when she looks at me.

'I just get the sense that Louise might be a bit dangerous.'

'Really, you think it's that bad?'

'Don't you?'

I have to think about that. My wife has never shown any signs of aggression. To be completely honest, she was the perfect partner until Abby turned up, but all levels of mental instability tend to have a catalyst. Not that it's my field, but I know people.

'Why don't you just stick it out for a few more days?' I suggest. 'Things might change, you might land a nice job somewhere here in the village, and you can start making your own money. I can help you with a new place to live, and maybe then Louise might calm down a bit. You know, because you won't be in her territory as such.'

'And if something else happens in the meantime?'

'I'll keep an eye out for you.'

'You promise?'

'Cross my heart.'

Abby smiles and leans over to hug me. I embrace her as I always have, holding her tight to let her know her big brother will always be here for her, no matter what. The problem is I just can't shake the book out of my thoughts. Something isn't quite right, and although I tell myself it's not a good time to bring it up, there won't be a better time.

'Now that's out of the way, I have a question of my own.'

Abby peels away, hangs her legs over mine, then scoots back. 'What's that?'

'The book you gave me for my birthday—'

'Do you not like it?'

'No, I love it. It's just that it's something Louise might have given me.'

Everything I need to know is in her reaction. The hurt, the betrayal, and the resignation to the idea that we could all be happy here. 'I had a feeling this would happen,' she says. 'Look, I didn't have a gift for you because I have no money. That's what it's like when you just come out of prison. I told Louise that I felt guilty, so she said I can take *her* gift and say it's from me. I'm so sorry. I really wanted to get you something you'd love.'

'Hey, I do love it, no matter who it's from.'

'But now you think I'm a liar.'

'No, not at all. It's a white lie.'

To be honest, it's kind of a relief. I knew something was wrong, but I didn't truly believe I'd find out what. I'm so proud of Abby for coming forward and telling me the truth, and the fact Louise didn't forget to buy me something is a nice bonus. No matter who the book is technically from, I'll cherish it forever.

My stress levels have been on a roller coaster this past half hour, and I'm just about done. I tell Abby this, and she suggests I lie down for a bit. It doesn't take much convincing, so I stretch my legs out, but she doesn't move. I playfully kick her, and then she finally adjusts her position so we're top and tail Just like when we were younger, when life was a game and we didn't have a care in the world.

She dozes within a minute, her light snoring making me laugh at first, but I soon find melody in it. It's like a lullaby to me, all those years of sharing a room coming back to me in an instant. I love her so much, and I'm so glad she's home.

It calms me so much that, finally, I can sleep.

I WAKE UP WITH A WEAK, groggy body and a weird taste in my mouth. Abby's feet are tucked under my chin, the cotton of her socks surprisingly rough and damp with sweat. I swipe them away gently and sit up without disturbing her, looking at the clock above my desk. An hour has passed, and it's going to take a whole lot of coffee to wake me up.

It's not like I can carry on working anyway since Abby is out like a light in my only home office. I'm starting to regret choosing a computer over a laptop because that would have enabled me to simply take my tasks into another room, perhaps even a café or a park bench. Anywhere that isn't here, basically.

Louise passes me on the stairs, Mia asleep in her arms. She mouths to me that she needs to talk, then heads into the nursery to put Mia down for an afternoon nap. I nod and continue down the stairs, wondering when the nightmare of being stuck in the middle will end. I'm already frustrated enough without having to bear additional weight. Sometime, it has to stop.

With that said, I do want to give her the benefit of the doubt. It's obvious she's been trying really hard lately, and with her appointment lurking just around the corner, I have a little faith that our marriage will survive.

A little, but not much.

Downstairs, a pot of coffee is already made up and half gone. I pour myself a small cup, leaving enough for two others should they need it, then go to the back window and gaze out upon our large, luscious garden. There's a farmer's field on the other end of it, but that's blocked off by a fence I can barely see because of the full, healthy trees. It's paradise, and I should be making more of an effort to stay out there in the sun. There's just so little free time that I don't really get to relax, much less in the summer when everyone in the village is going out and spreading bugs just so they can stay under the summer sun.

'Is now a good time?'

Louise appears behind me. I turn to face her, instantly noticing the phone in her hand. She has it poised like she wants to show me something on it. I'm already starting to panic that another drama is about to unravel, but it's only fair to give her a chance.

'As long as it doesn't take too long. I'm still working.'

'That all depends on your answer to my question.'

'Which is?'

She turns the phone towards me, and my past comes back to hit me like a brick out of the great blue sky. There's a face I never thought I'd see again, attached to a name I thought I left behind. But it's all right there in front of me, demanding an explanation.

'Do you know this person?' she asks, and I can tell she's heard something – some rubbish about what I've done in a previous life or a justice that needs to be balanced. Louise stares at me, patiently waiting to learn whether I know Joanna Heywood. And I certainly do.

How could I forget?

Chapter 17
Louise

I GOT the message last night, right on the tail end of Daniel's birthday dinner. Acting as though it never happened was one of the hardest things I've ever had to do. I didn't want to ruin his birthday, and I certainly didn't want to disturb him while he was in the middle of work, but I know for a fact he took the time to speak with Abby.

So now he has to speak with me.

Daniel is staring at the screen. It's unclear what he's thinking, but there are definitely some strong emotions dwelling within his eyes. Bad ones, too, as if that comes as any kind of surprise. From what I've read, he already knows a lot about the woman on my phone.

'That's Joanna Heywood,' he says.

'Go on,' I tell him, as if he has something to answer for.

'She's no longer in our lives.'

'*Our* lives?'

'Abby and I.' He points at the screen. 'This woman. She...'

Is that the first sign of a tear I see, or is that just my mind wanting it to be there? Because from what the message said last night, he absolutely should hate to hear from Joanna. They have a very dramatic past that is already proving itself true by the way Daniel avoids looking again. Instead, his eyes are locked on mine, staring deep into my soul.

'I don't know what to tell you, but this woman is trouble.'

'Care to elaborate on that?'

'Maybe. What did she tell you?'

I shake my head to tell him that, no, he's not going to get the answer from me. First, he has to tell me his side of the story. I want to see if the two tales align or how drastically different they are. There's something in the way he stands, crossing his arms. There's *something*...

'It's not really me she has the problem with. It's Abby.' Daniel sighs heavily. 'Remember I said she was in prison for killing someone with her car? Her name was Anita Heywood. Joanna is her sister, and she's... Last time I saw her, she...'

'You can tell me.' I lower my phone because I can see it's causing him pain.

'As Abby was heading into the courthouse for trial, Joanna threw a glass bottle at her. It missed, thank God, but I'll never forget the way Joanna screamed. She was hurting, as you can expect from losing a sister, but she insisted Abby had killed Anita on purpose.'

I want to ask if she did, because – honestly – it wouldn't surprise me. But I know better than to put forward such an accusation. Especially to Daniel, who must have already heard more than enough between me and his sister. I let him continue.

'After Abby was sentenced, I started being followed by someone in a red Fiesta. It took weeks for me to get a glimpse of the number plate. When I did, I gave it a search online and found out it belonged to—'

'Joanna?'

'Right.'

'So, what became of it?'

'Absolutely nothing. Time went by, and she stopped long enough to let me breathe. Remember,

I was struggling, too. My sister had just gone to prison for vehicular manslaughter. It tore us apart. This little slice of me that belonged to a family was gone, and now I was being hounded for her mistake. I understood, obviously, but that didn't make it right.'

I stare back at my husband, suddenly understanding him a little more. His devotion to Abby clearly comes from some misplaced sense of loyalty. Abby made a mistake, sure, but that was *her* mistake. It was never Daniel's burden to bear.

'What did Joanna say to you?' he asks, rubbing his eye before checking his watch.

'That Abby is trouble.'

'I suppose she would think that.'

'Thank you for telling me.'

'It's okay.'

He takes a deep breath and then laughs aloud at how heavy things have become. I laugh with him, slightly through relief that I know Joanna a little more than I did five minutes ago. Back when the world seemed so small and dismal that I almost didn't want to be a part of it.

Daniel kisses me on the lips, smiles, then takes a mug of coffee back up to work. I'm alone downstairs now, with a couple of hours to spare while

Mia snoozes and Abby is out of the way. Normally I'd use this opportunity to sleep, but how can I when I just lied to my husband?

The message said more than what I told him. Not much more in terms of word count, but the severity of those words has already sunk into my brain, throwing a spanner in the works of an already complicated situation. I take a seat in the kitchen and ponder the message Joanna sent me last night, taking my phone out to read it once more.

Stay away from Abby Wright. She's psychotic.

I've sent her a reply and am I waiting patiently to hear back. I want to learn more about what she knows. Until then, I'll just waste time going over the facts in my head.

Daniel told me long ago what happened the night of the accident. It was dark and icy, the roads slippery as hell. Daniel had been out on the town to celebrate his first real job as a doctor, and he needed a lift home. Abby was there for him, as she always had been, picking him up from a bar at two in the morning and driving him home safely.

Except it wasn't safe.

There's a blind turning just outside of their hometown, and Abby took it carefully. She admitted many times to being exhausted that night, and she just couldn't react fast enough when Anita Heywood came speeding around the bend. Their cars connected with a metallic smack. Abby lost control of the vehicle, while Anita's car ploughed through a barricade and off a steep hill, where it rolled multiple times, killing her almost instantly.

Nobody believed Anita was speeding, despite Daniel's testimony, so Abby was sentenced to ten years in prison. Daniel fell into a deep depression at the start of her sentence, but he carried on with his life nonetheless. That's how he was when I met him: holding it together, but barely.

There's a ton of different reasons I married the man I met. Nobody has a straightforward life, and I was more than prepared to accept him despite how down in the dumps he was. No matter how he felt, he always got out of bed and put in the time, even though he missed his sister so dearly. To this day, I wonder if he blames himself. If he hadn't been out on the town, Abby never would have been on the road. Anita would still be alive, and all would be perfect.

Except I never would have met him.

The Sister-in-Law

I was in London, visiting an old friend for the weekend, when I sprained my ankle running for the Tube. I screamed and hit the floor, but nobody cared. Nobody, apart from Daniel. He was in the city for similar reasons, and he stopped to help me to my feet. We got talking and quickly found out that we really liked each other. It was one of those whirlwind romances – it swept us off our feet in a heartbeat, and four years later, we're married with the most beautiful baby in the entire world.

So at least something came from his misery.

Over the years, he started to perk up, but I've never seen him happier than the day he found out Abby was being released early for good behaviour. He came home from work, bursting through the door with a smile so big I thought his skin was about to tear.

'She's coming out!' he yelled, grabbing me. 'She's being released!'

If I knew back then how this would all turn out, I would've suggested she stayed somewhere else. The problem is that I didn't have a clue she would turn out to be a psycho. Now, as I sit here staring at Joanna's profile picture, I wonder if Abby has always been this way. Or was it something that came from life on the inside?

I'll never know, I suppose. This whole thing is wearing me down. Every time I think things will be okay, something new pops up out of nowhere. I was actually willing to see out the two weeks while I wait for my psychiatrist's appointment, but now that Joanna has thrown her voice into the mix, it's hard not to pay attention to her advice. I know for a fact Abby is toxic, but proving it is the real challenge.

So, am I supposed to try? Or am I better off just coasting by until she finally gets a job and moves away? The latter is a nice dream, but in reality, it feels like she's never going to get out of here. Why would she when she has everything so perfectly laid out for her?

I'm ready to scream from all the overthinking. All I want is to curl up on the bed and get some rest while Mia allows it. I might even give it a try, despite the storm raging in my mind, so I get up from the kitchen chair and head for the stairs.

I stop when I see Abby.

'Is there a problem?' she asks, standing in the doorway.

In *my* way.

'No,' I tell her, stepping aside to give her a chance to move. 'No problem at all.'

As she passes, I want to tell her that I know. That Joanna has been in contact with me, and now there's a second person who doesn't think I should trust my own sister-in-law. It's actually kind of liberating. I've spent so long thinking I'm crazy – as if everyone thinks Abby is perfect – that even I was starting to believe it. See, Joanna knows something.

I just don't know what yet.

Abby squints like she doesn't trust me, then goes to the main hall and grabs her handbag. Now that I'm full of confidence, I see no reason not to follow her. Maybe even *challenge* her on where she's going and what she's up to. I'm in half a mind to call her on what she did to me about Daniel's birthday present, but there's one thing I must remind myself.

One thing at a time.

'Where are you off to?' I ask, watching her put on sunglasses.

She checks herself out in the hallway mirror, pouting like she thinks the sun shines out of her... well, you get the idea. 'Me? I'm going to meet a friend in the village. Is that okay, or should I have asked your permission first?'

'Do what you want.'

'Good. I will.'

Abby turns her back on me, but not before looking down her nose at me first. I know what's happening here: I'm asking questions she doesn't want me asking, and she's confused by my new bout of confidence. She's been so comfortable walking all over me that she didn't expect me to say anything about her leaving.

But she better get used to it.

Because I'm on to her.

She furrows her brow with confusion, then walks right out the front door. I close it because she couldn't be bothered, then stand with my back against the thick wood. This is the perfect opportunity to do something, I realise. With Daniel back at work and Abby heading into the village, I'm actually in a position to follow her.

But I shouldn't...

Should I?

The first thing I do is hurry into the living room and check the monitor. Mia is stirring in her cot. If I'm quick, there's no reason I can't get her into the buggy and take after Abby. I do this as quickly as possible, sparing her my playful nature that she usually wakes up to, heading out the door with her as though the house is about to explode.

Abby doesn't have friends. I know this because

Daniel told me so many times. Even if she did, she wouldn't know a single soul in Dolcester. So what exactly is she up to? Where is she going that she doesn't want me or Daniel to know about?

I'm about to find out.

Chapter 18
Daniel

I'M NO FOOL. I've seen Abby leave, and Louise went out shortly after. She's following her. She must be. But at least this leaves me in the house alone, trying desperately to calm down after learning that Joanna is trying to involve herself in my life once again. I'm so tired of this, having to go over the same old ground again and again. Is it too much to ask for a break?

There's no way I'm working now. I'm simply not in the mood. Although I didn't show it at the time, Louise has me seething after shoving the phone in my face and demanding an explanation. I never lied to her – never had a reason to either – so it disgusted me to see how quickly she came in with an accusation. More than anything, I'm shocked at how quickly she accepted the truth and moved on.

Something isn't right there.

As soon as all three of them are out of sight from my office window, I shut down the computer and start packing up. I don't even mean to slam the doors like this, but I'm wound up so tight that I'm just about ready to scream.

It's time to call an emergency meeting.

Truth be told, I don't have much in the way of friends. There are people I've examined and treated since I officially became one of the only two doctors here, and some of them have sworn they owe me a debt they can never repay. That's not why I did it – I did it because I care about my profession as much as the people I train to help – but I'm in desperate need of conversation from someone who doesn't live under my roof.

John Williams – not *that* one – is the first on my list, a man who once came to me with an ear infection that turned out to be caused by a brain tumour. I had him fast-tracked to surgery, and the surgeons there saved his life. As were his words: he owes me one.

Carl Jennings is next. He once came to me out of hours with a dog that got hit by a car. The village vet was on holiday at the time, so there was nobody to turn to but me. I told him I couldn't guarantee the poor pooch's survival, and he signed a waiver to let me operate. The dog made it, and in his own words: he owes me one.

Lastly, there's Dr. Jeremy Phillips. This man is my colleague and doesn't owe me a thing, but he plays poker with John and Carl every other Thursday. If I invite them to come and talk with me, he'll have to come, too. That's fine by me – it can't hurt to have another voice in my ear. After all, I'm a big boy, so I can make my own decision at the end of it.

It's just their opinions that interest me.

They all report back by way of text message, telling me to meet them at the local pub for a pint and a chat. I pause just long enough to decide if this is the right thing to do as I don't want my personal life out there in the public eye. When I realise there's nothing else I can do, I type out my replies and agree to meet them in just a few minutes.

I should be back before anyone realises I'm gone.

. . .

THE WHITE LION is the only pub in the village. It has a comfortable Tudor theme and is a little cramped inside, so the guys are waiting for me in the beer garden. The last time I was here, Abby and I enjoyed our food together and then went home to a furious Louise. It's not a memory I want to relive, so I'm glad a table is reserved at the other end of the garden.

It's nice and quiet for late afternoon, with only a small family creating noise a few tables away. The parents are young, both playing with their phones while their kids run rampant around the grass, knocking into the staff who come to clear up empty glasses. I hate to see things like this – how hard is it to be present when your kids are involved?

Speaking of which, I swallow my hypocrisy and sit down with my friends while Louise is out with our child. John hands me a pint of Guinness. Jeremy watches me while Carl ends his story about how much the mechanic charged him for his MOT.

'Thanks for coming,' I say, and I can tell they're ready to listen because they all go silent. As I'm readying myself to tell the story, it occurs to me that if Dr. Phillips is here, then there's no doctor left at the surgery. 'Aren't you supposed to be working?'

'Aren't you?' Jeremy laughs. 'My last appointment was this morning. We closed on time for once. But enough about me. Come on, what's got your panties in a twist?'

I look around the table and wonder just how much I can trust these guys. I called them my friends, but they're really just the closest thing I have. I can count on one hand the number of times I've exposed my personal life to them. Hell, I can do it on one finger because until now, my life in Dolcester has been pretty peachy.

There's been nothing to tell until today.

So I give them the full story, going as far back as Abby's car accident. The years in between aren't important, so I gloss over those and get right to the juicy stuff. Which is to say the problems caused between my wife and sister. As I tell my story, I'm ashamed to say I get a little choked up. It's then that I realise the severity of my problems – things have gone from bad to worse in such a short space of time that I don't know what to do any more.

And that's exactly what I tell them.

By the time I've finished talking, all three of them are blowing out air in an exaggerated fashion, but the stress behind it is genuine. There's not a person on earth who could hear my tale and not feel engrossed by the same strains as mine.

'The first thing I want to ask,' John says, 'is what do *you* want to do about it?'

'I just want them to get on, but honestly, it doesn't look like it will happen.'

'Then you'll need to take that off the table and think of other solutions.'

That much is obvious, but I don't say anything, instead favouring my drink. I take a long gulp of it like it's water, and the cold ale falls down my throat too easily. A quarter of the pint is gone in a single swallow without me even trying. I'll blame the heat.

'Can't the professional see Louise sooner?' Carl asks.

'Apparently not. Who knew Dolcester could keep a shrink so busy?'

'You know what it's like in the healthcare field out here,' Jeremy says, picking his nails. 'We all moved here because we wanted a slower and steadier life. Whoever Louise is planning to see, they probably only work part-time. A couple of hours three days a week, or something like that. It's not very helpful, but you can't blame them for that.'

'I'm not blaming them,' I explain. 'Just wishing it was different.'

'What if the professional doesn't help matters?' Carl asks.

I shrug. 'It will have to end in divorce.'

The table goes silent then, as if they've already discussed this and are in wordless agreement with each other. They exchange looks before John finally speaks up. 'You would trust your sister over your own wife?'

'Shouldn't I? We've known each other for longer.'

'I'm just making sure *you* know what you want. We've all met Abby, and she seems lovely. Louise does, too, but she's lived here all this time, and we barely know her. I hate to admit it, but I suppose it's more likely Abby is telling the truth. Even if that does make Louise the villain in your own marriage. Although I must say I'm surprised.'

I was afraid they'd think that. Call it denial if you like, but I was really hoping these friends of mine might side with Louise – that I'd be crazy to leave such a wonderful woman. The question is, is she *really* wonderful, or was that all an act leading up to Abby's arrival?

'You really think Louise is lying?' I ask.

John nods hesitantly, so I look at Carl and Jeremy, who both nod and then reach for their drinks in perfect synchronisation. This is a very painful way to learn that nobody trusts my wife, even though I've tried to be fair and tell the story from a level playing field. I didn't give them the bias towards Abby – they reached that on their own.

Just like I did, although it took me days to figure it out.

There's little left to say on the matter, so I thank them and change the subject. The guys turn to football as a conversational topic, but I never really cared for the sport, so I just sit there and pretend to listen while I finish my drink. Not that I hear much of what they're saying.

I'm too deep in thought to care.

I TAKE the long way home, trying to enjoy the scenery of fields and flower-filled gardens some of the elderly have been tending to over the summer. The sun is on my back, drawing a sweat as the

Guinness takes its toll on me already. I never was much of a drinker – it's not that I don't enjoy it, but it unlocks freedom in my head and causes me to overthink.

As if my brain could get any messier right now.

I keep going over what the guys said about Abby. It's not that I didn't have doubts about her side of the story, but it always seemed unlikely that she would be causing trouble in my home. Louise, on the other hand, has every reason to feel defensive. I'll never forget the way she looked at me when I excitedly told her my sister was being released from prison. It was the face of someone who really couldn't care less. A look that said, *'Good for you. Now, may I please continue reading my magazine?'*

It's not like I expected her to care as much as I did, but of course, I noticed an immediate disinterest. I see that face everywhere I go on my way home: as I stroll through the meandering alleys to extend my walk; through the park, where kids are running and shouting without a care in the world; all the way along the long stretch of road leading up to our house. It's becoming something of a headache, although the blazing sun must be partially responsible for that.

Getting home should feel like a relief because it's cool inside and offers salvation from the sweltering summer heat. But all I can think about is the worsening situation I'm in. It makes me feel a little sick, if I'm honest. I've loved Louise since the moment I met her, but the more I learn about her, the less interested I am in continuing a life like this. Aren't spouses supposed to take you *and* your family? Isn't it a package deal?

Speaking of which, where is she? I haven't seen a sign of her or Abby since they left the house suspiciously close together. I can imagine they'll both be coming home in a short while, at each other's throats as usual. In the meantime, I have some pretty big life-altering decisions to make regarding my future. I don't want Mia to grow up in a broken home.

But Louise is making it harder every day.

Our marriage is officially on its last legs.

Chapter 19
Louise

Just when I thought Abby couldn't wind me up any more, she's taking her precious time going where she wants to go. Initially, when she sat outside the café and slowly sipped on a bottle of water, I thought she just wanted to come out and get some air.

But then I looked a little closer.

Her hands were trembling.

Twenty minutes or so are spent there, and finally, she's on the move. I've taken cover behind a weeping willow, concealing myself behind the tree's trunk. Mia is playful in her buggy, facing me with the most adoring eyes the world has ever seen. I desperately want to stop and play with her, but right now, I'm trying to find out what Abby's doing.

Because it just might save my marriage.

As she walks on, I step on to the pavement, following as closely as I can while she heads down the semi-busy cobblestone road Dolcester dares to call a high street. There are only three shops and a café – two of those are charity shops, the other a newsagent – so this many villagers shouldn't be walking around out here. I'm not normally overwhelmed by people, but so much is at stake that my heart is starting to flutter.

Thankfully, Abby doesn't look back as she crosses the road. I'm starting to see how she managed to crash a car into an unsuspecting driver, given how careless and unaware of her surroundings she is. Daniel would say that line of thinking is mean, but what does he know?

He can't even see the pure evil right in front of him.

As Abby rounds the corner and disappears from sight, I take a quick look at both ends of the road and then cross over. Some people move out of my way, looking annoyed as they sidestep me on my mission to discover whatever this is all about. Others are more stubborn, blocking my path until I ask them to move. They eventually do, parting in the crowd to reveal someone I badly didn't want to bump into today.

'Hi, Louise.'

Lisa is standing in my path, her blonde but greying hair matted to her forehead with sweat. She's suffering from the heat just like the rest of us, and it seems she thinks small talk is the answer to her troubles.

I don't have time for this.

'Sorry, Lisa. I have to go.'

'Oh, running late?'

'Something like that.'

'How did things go with the sister-in-law?'

'Not great. That's actually where I'm—'

'Ah, sorry.'

Lisa steps out of my way, and I feel awful for rushing past her. I wouldn't go so far as to call her a friend, but she's been kind enough to talk to me about my problems on more than one occasion. I owe her, quite frankly, and maybe I'll repay that debt someday.

But right now, I have other things going on.

I rush towards the corner, Mia giggling at my sudden burst of speed as the buggy rattles over the uneven pavement. I smile falsely at her, suddenly panicking that I've missed my opportunity. When I

The Sister-in-Law

turn on to the next street, Abby is nowhere in sight. There are just three people walking together – one of whom is Daniel's colleague at the surgery.

'Hi, Louise,' one of them says.

I smile and hurry past, mostly because I've forgotten all of their names. They clear a space for me to move, and I thank them because whatever I do next could easily be reported back to my husband. It's the last thing I want, but what other choice do I have?

Abby absolutely mustn't get away from me.

Luckily, I find her on the next street over. She waits at a bus stop, so I linger on the corner right in direct sunlight. At least Mia has some shade, so I give her a snack to keep her mouth busy while I watch for over ten minutes. Nothing happens with Abby – nothing at all.

Not until the bus comes.

I'm not sure what I'm seeing, but I know it's not good.

The old man who steps off the bus is portly, aged somewhere in his early- to mid-sixties, with a flowing ash-grey beard tinted yellow with cigarette smoke. The moment the bus is gone, Abby stands and approaches, wringing her hands together as she looks him dead in the eye. I can't hear what they're saying from my hiding spot on the corner, but – judging by the unease between them and the way both their hands are shaking – I'm sure it's not good.

After a minute or so of talking, they begin to walk back in my direction. Panicking, I step back into a quiet lane and pray they walk past. As luck would have it, they do, and I even hear a quick snippet of their conversation.

'He doesn't know?' the man asks, his voice booming and echoing down the lane.

It's Abby's voice next, unmistakably: 'No, he doesn't have a clue.'

'Good. Let's keep it that way.'

Their voices fall to mutters as they gain distance from me. Mia finishes her snacks and makes a cute but thankfully short sound as she signs for more food. I haven't been teaching her sign language, but she's picking up a couple of things from the shows I leave on for her while I keep her in her playpen and run to the bathroom. Not my proudest move, but often necessary.

I give her another treat just to keep her quiet, then step out of the lane. Abby and the man are still in sight, but they've stopped on the side of the street. I sneak back to where I was, peering around the corner as sneakily as possible to see what happens next.

It comes out of nowhere.

Abby lowers her head and starts to sob. I can't hear it – can't even see it in great detail from this distance – but it's evident in the way her shoulders bob up and down. The old man doesn't hesitate in spreading his arms and taking her in for a long, hard hug.

I know this is wrong, but I can't help myself. Without so much as a second thought, I take my phone out and snap a few pictures of the hug. It's too intimate for my liking, and although she's free to live her own life, I don't like what I've heard from her.

'No, he doesn't have a clue.'

Whatever it is they're talking about, I'm certain it's nothing good. Maybe that's why it seems like such a good idea to get the photographic evidence. Not just so I can later clarify I wasn't seeing things but also to obtain proof that she did meet a stranger in town today.

And there's no way she can deny it.

. . .

I GET HOME long before Abby does, which gives me time to feed Mia and then get comfortable. Daniel is upstairs now – I can hear him tapping away at his computer keyboard – but there's no need to disturb him just yet. Besides, it might be fun to have a little communication with my rival first, letting her know she's been seen having strange rendezvous.

It's actually a pretty long wait. I can only assume she's spending more time with that man, which gives me a little space to wonder what that was all about. I keep thinking back to the conversation, wondering just who 'he' was and what 'he doesn't have a clue' about. It wouldn't surprise me if they were talking about Daniel.

But I guess we'll soon know for sure.

Mia is happy playing on her own when Abby walks in the front door. I can hear her kicking off those ugly heels she likes to wear, then shuffling her grotty socks across the floor to look in the living room. She sees me and says nothing, but when Mia spots her and eagerly crawls over to her, Abby's face lights up as she drops to the floor for a big hug. I won't lie – it kills me to see my own baby love that monster of a woman so much.

'Good day?' I ask, starting a conversation so I

can segue into something much more fun. There's no point denying how good it feels to finally have one over on her. Even if Abby does ignore me, focusing on making Mia squirm and giggle with tickles.

I try again. 'Good day on your own? Assuming, of course, you were on your own.'

That's enough to make her stop tickling my daughter and glare at me from across the room. Her smile vanishes in the blink of an eye, a scowl now in its place. Before she says anything, she picks up Mia and puts her in front of her books, making her look up with a confused frown. Abby, meanwhile, comes to stand over me.

An intimidation tactic, for sure.

'What are you trying to suggest?' she asks bluntly.

'Suggesting? Absolutely nothing. I'm *telling* you I know all about it.'

'There's nothing to know.'

'Oh, I think there is.' It's not like me to try acting tough, but it's too deliciously fun to have Abby sweating. I push myself to my feet and stand chest to chest with her, giving her what I can only describe as a death stare. 'You should start looking around a bit more when you go for walks. You never know who might be following you. It could be someone who hates you. Can you imagine what would happen if someone like that saw you meeting strange men? It would completely mess with your little game, wouldn't it?'

Abby doesn't say a word. Her eyes do all the talking: panic, fear, and... upset?

'You can speak,' I say, mostly because I don't feel comfortable in her silence. 'In fact, the more you say, the better it might look when Daniel finds out about this.'

'There's nothing to tell.' She shrugs, but I know she cares. 'I didn't meet anyone.'

'Is that right? What if I told you there's photographic evidence to prove it?'

'Please tell me you didn't—'

'I also overheard your conversation. So, Daniel doesn't have a clue, does he? And that old man you were meeting, he wants to keep it that way, right?' I'm bluffing my way through this, leaving just enough for her to take the conversation and say something she shouldn't. Something that might implicate her for everything she's done. 'Well? Want to tell me who the old man was and what you were meeting him for?'

Abby's eyes are alert and angry. I've got her – I know it, she knows it.

'Now you listen here,' she says, jabbing a finger into my rib so hard that it makes me gasp and step back. She comes forward then, putting me on my heels as I walk back towards the wall. Mia starts screaming, and I faintly hear footsteps on the stairs. 'My business is *my* business, and I won't have some pathetic stay-at-home mum follow me around town. Give me your phone right now, or I'll prise it from your broken fingers, so help me G—'

'What's going on here?'

Daniel appears in the doorway. No sooner does Mia stop crying than Abby starts. It's terrifying how quickly she switches from furious to heartbroken, tears instantly forming in her eyes as her face turns red. She blubbers like an upset schoolgirl, making Daniel come in and put an arm around her shoulders.

'What's the matter?' he asks.

Abby shoves away his arm and storms off, turning up the volume on her fake sobbing so the whole house can hear. I'm absolutely blown away by the audacity that woman has, manipulating my husband so expertly that he can't even see it.

Well, he's about to. Now that I have proof of

her strange comings and goings on my phone, there's little she can do. It's not much – meeting a man in town hardly makes her the bad guy – but when you pair it with the rest of her strange activity, it lends a little credibility to the story I've been trying to tell Daniel all along.

All I need is for him to hear me out. I'm already reaching for my phone, my hands all shaky from my violent interaction with his dear, sweet sister. By the time it's out of my pocket and I've unlocked it, however, he's no longer standing in front of me.

Abby is his priority now.

Chapter 20
Daniel

AFTER GETTING BACK from talking with my friends, I found a little distraction in my work. There really wasn't much to do, so I set about rewriting some notes to make them clearer. This occupied both my mind and my fingers, the latter pattering around the keys so fast there was simply no time to think about how bad my life had become.

Shortly after, there was a ruckus downstairs. These walls are nice and thick, but they don't keep out *every* sound. There was enough muffled talking to pull me out of my work and send me downstairs, where Louise was picking on Abby once again, and Mia was screeching at the top of her lungs as a reaction to whatever it was she saw.

Looking at Louise now, I can't believe I've let things come this far. Her hands are shaking with rage, my sister having disappeared upstairs to get away from the poor treatment. I don't know what's happened or why, but I'll find out from Abby any minute now.

I leave the room but barely make it to the stairs. Louise comes launching out of the living room, stopping in the doorway so she can keep an eye on Mia. But her attention isn't on our daughter – it's on me and the phone she's trying to show me for the second time today.

'What now?' I ask a little too harshly, but with good reason.

'Recognise her?'

'Should I?'

I've barely looked at the screen, mostly because I'm too angry to care about what silly little story my wife has now concocted. When I see the pleading in her eyes, I exhale loudly and finally look at the screen, using my fingers to zoom in. I don't know what to feel when I see a picture of Abby standing at a bus stop, but it's definitely not good.

'What am I looking at?' I say, trying to hold back my rage.

'It's Abby. She's been in town meeting someone.'

'Right? Is she not allowed to see people?'

'Of course she is, but she said she doesn't know anyone in Dolcester.'

'Louise, she's at the bus stop, for crying out loud. You know, the place where people arrive from different locations after travelling?'

'No.' She shakes her head rapidly, taking none of this. 'You don't understand. She hugged him, then I overheard them talking about a secret.'

It takes everything I have not to sigh. 'What are you talking about?'

'I didn't want them to see me, so I ducked into a lane—'

'Jesus.'

'Seriously, listen. I overheard them talking about how you don't know something. And the old man said they should try to keep it that way. Look, I know this doesn't exactly tell us *what* she's up to, but she's definitely up to *something*. You must see that.'

Of all the things to expect out of today, this wasn't one of them. Things have been rough enough lately without Louise following Abby into town and taking photos of her. I'm inclined to give her a piece of my mind for even doing it in the first place, but as I stare into her eyes, I see she truly, strongly believes she's found something worth exploring.

It's not right, but I want to entertain her just enough to feel like I'm not doing something wrong by automatically siding with my sister. It's probably not easy for Louise either – I know she's getting help soon and intends to actually work on this paranoia of hers, but I can't dismiss her feelings entirely. Besides, I am slightly curious about who the old man in the picture is.

And what they're both hiding from me.

'All right,' I say, resigning to her plea. 'I'm going to head upstairs and talk to her. Just promise me you won't come up screaming at her and making everything worse. She's finding her adjustment from prison difficult enough without this conflict.'

Louise looks like she wants to hit me. It's the same look she gave me in the other room, right after I caught her making Abby cry. I wonder what was said between them to make things get so heated. Whatever it was, I get the impression Louise isn't telling me everything.

Which is fair, because we both know I wouldn't believe her anyway.

I FIND ABBY UPSTAIRS, face down on the bed in her room. She only briefly glances up at me as I enter, then returns to bury her face under her arms. I hate to see her like this, especially when it's my own wife that caused these tears in the first place.

But I did promise to look into this.

'Why don't you tell me your side of the events?' I say, feeling like a parent investigating a row between my two kids. I take a seat on the bed, ready to listen to a lengthy story about how this whole thing exploded.

It doesn't happen.

'There's nothing to tell.' Abby wipes her tears, sniffles, then sits upright and hugs her knees. She looks a little like she did when we were kids – innocent, vulnerable, and afraid. 'I went into town, and Louise followed me. When I got back, she started accusing me of meeting up with some creep. Then she told me she would—'

'Did you?'

'Did I what?'

'Whether or not he's a creep, did you meet someone?'

Abby stares at me blankly, then shakes her head. This is the real kicker for me because now I know she's capable of lying to me. There's a swirl of confusing emotions raging around inside my head, not knowing who to believe or what to do about it.

'I've seen the photo, sis. You're lying to me.'

'It's not like that.' Abby wipes her cheeks dry again, then sits back and crosses her legs. She looks me right in the eye, but her head is hanging low as if she's ashamed of what she's about to tell me. 'The man I met was my cellmate's father. I called him from your landline when you were out the other day, asking if I could meet with him face to face.'

This doesn't make any sense. 'Why would you do that?'

'Because she made me promise to give him something.'

'Give him what exactly?'

'A note. Something she wrote the morning she killed herself.'

I see it then, clear as day. A real, genuine tear rolling down her cheek the same way raindrops slide down glass. She smears it away with her knuckle, then goes on.

'She was stuck in there for life and couldn't bear the weight of it any more. Seeing as I was leaving and her dad didn't want to visit her in prison, she wanted to say her last words to him. When we met, I gave him the note and talked with him for a while. It was closure for the both of them. And me, I suppose.'

'That's all you were doing? Passing on a note?'

'What else would I be up to?' Abby points towards the door as if Louise is standing behind me. She's not. '*She* followed me through the village and took photos of me like some paranoid weirdo. I'm getting so sick of this.'

'So am I,' I confess. 'What about the things Louise overheard?'

Abby shakes her head, as confused as I am.

'Something about how I'm not supposed to know and how he wants to keep it that way.'

'Is that what she told you we said?'

'Do you deny it?'

'No, it's just taken out of context.' She gets up and crosses the room, staring out of the open window as if watching something. A soft breeze creeps through and ruffles her hair, suddenly making her look like a princess on her royal balcony. 'The man we were talking about was my cellmate's brother. He's backpacking across Europe at the moment, completely unaware that his sister is dead. Their dad doesn't want to tell him until he's home.'

I sit for a moment to take it all in. For once, I actually understand the confusion. Mostly because I've been a part of it ever since the two of them got through the door. I'll explain all of this to Louise, of course, all while trying to decide if I should be angry with her or not.

'You hate me for this, don't you?' Abby asks.

'Why would I hate you?'

'Because it's caused another problem.'

'No, it's just... more drama, you know?'

Abby nods, but she doesn't speak. I can see another tear working its way towards her chin, and I start to wonder just how much more of this she can take. Even *I'm* reaching my limit, starting to question once again if Louise and I can get through this. Things seem to be getting tougher every day, and with new problems arising every time I turn around, I should be asking myself if this is it.

If this is the end of our marriage.

. . .

I HATE to sound like I know what's best for my wife, but it wouldn't surprise me if her tiredness of being the primary caregiver is affecting her mental state. I've come downstairs and told her to take the rest of the evening to herself because if she can rest up and maybe start seeing more clearly, it might make life easier for the rest of us.

This is so desperate, I realise as I hold open some lift-the-flap books for Mia. But looking at the precious little bundle of joy in my life, I feel a desperate need to prevent this house from becoming a hostile environment. Just seeing the rivalry between her mother and Abby must be extremely confusing for her – it certainly is for me – so trust me when I say I'll do absolutely anything to clear the air between them.

Mia pulls back the cardboard tractor in the book and reveals some ducks in a field. She squeals with pure joy and points at them, making a noise that sounds sort of like 'quack'. Seeing my baby girl so happy puts things into perspective.

'That's right,' I tell her. 'Quack-quack.'

She giggles at my noise and beak-hand, then turns the pages. I really am the luckiest man in the world. Some bad times just happen to have fallen on us, that's all. I'm trying to convince myself everything is going to work out if I can just hang in there until Louise sees the doctor. Not that it will ever really solve anything. She already proved she's not changing.

Why else would she follow Abby?

A couple of hours pass, and Louise comes downstairs to take over. She fell asleep and is quite rested, she says, then asks what happened with Abby. I tell her everything about the man she met and what exactly they were talking about. Louise frowns as if I'm crazy – like nothing could be further from the truth – but the facts are right there whether she wants to accept them or not. And judging by her expression, I'm guessing not.

That's as far as the conversation goes because I don't have the energy to go through this crap again. Every time we talk, it feels like I'm hiking through thick mud with the elements against me as I try to proceed but keep being forced back. What's the point in trying any more when things are so bad? Why subject myself to more torture?

When I go upstairs, I should be going to bed, but I'm far too wired to sleep. Just to distract myself, I head back into the office and prepare to do a little more work. But barely any gets done because, before I know it, my fingers are hitting the keys and looking up a certain service. It starts as more of a curiosity – perhaps even a touch of forward preparation – but that quickly evolves into something more. A firm decision that needs acting on immediately.

I start my email to the divorce attorney.

Chapter 21
Louise

DANIEL SLEEPS on the sofa tonight, leaving me alone in the bed with my mind racing. I know all about the man Abby met in town now – I know who he is, what he came here for, and why she kept it such a secret from everyone under this roof.

It's because she's ashamed.

That's the thing I've noticed about Abby. She doesn't like to talk about prison because it makes her feel like just a regular old criminal. I can see it in her eyes whenever such things are even hinted at. I think back to when we were watching a crime drama – before all of this insanity got too far – and a detective visited one of the crooks he put away in prison. I looked over at Abby, noticing she'd gone red in the cheeks, and similar things have happened ever since. As much as I hate her, it's nothing to be ashamed of. We all make mistakes.

It just so happened that hers cost a life.

Morning comes, with the sun beaming through the horrendously thin curtains. It wakes me up, but I still spend some time staring at the lit-up wall and pondering where exactly my life is heading. Not so long ago, I had the perfect life that many would envy. Now, I'm getting bullied in my own home with a psychiatry appointment lurking around the corner.

What has happened to me?

It's not long before there's a gentle knock on the door. Daniel comes in, his thin smile so fake that it worries me instantly. I glance over at the baby monitor to find Mia still sleeping in her cot. Above the image of our perfect daughter, the digital clock says it's almost eight.

'I thought maybe we should talk,' he says.

'Not a bad idea. Is there a pot of coffee on?'

'Actually, can we talk outside? Maybe we could go for a walk.'

I study him then, wondering why he's acting so strangely. Daniel loves to go for walks, but never with me. It's usually something he reserves for days when he isn't working and takes Mia from me so I can have a break. Why the sudden change?

'We shouldn't wake Mia,' I say.

'It's okay. Abby said she'll take care of her.'

'But—' The look in his eyes says not to argue, so I don't. 'All right, let me get dressed.'

I meet him downstairs ten minutes later, wearing breathable jeans and a light top with vented pits. As soon as we're out the door, I realise it was a good decision because the heat is ridiculous for the UK. Still, it's not the biggest thing on my mind.

Abby is in the house alone with our child, which makes me feel sick.

Daniel and I walk down the long road towards the fields we used to hike through. The roadside trees offer a little shade as we walk in silence, not stopping until we reach the stile that leads into a field. It's too hot to go traipsing through the grass with no shade around for miles, so he stops with one foot on the wood, gazing out at the stunning scenery.

He doesn't even look at me when he delivers the blow.

'I think we should get a divorce.'

The words hit me like a lorry. I'm digging

down deep to find something to say, but my gut is wrenched, and my eyes are already blurring with tears. When I do manage to speak, it first comes out croaky and desperate.

'But we love each other.'

'We do,' Daniel says. 'We really do, but I can't live like this.'

'Is it because of Abby?'

'No, it's because of how you're *treating* Abby.'

'But I can fix it. Whatever you want me to do—'

'Louise, I've been trying so hard to make you listen to me. Perhaps you haven't been paying attention to how I've been feeling, but you've spent the past few days making it clear that you don't want to get along with my sister. Do you realise the position that puts me in?'

'I...' No, I didn't realise, but now it's hard to unsee. I know Daniel has been getting frustrated by all of this – we both have – but if I knew things were so bad that he can't stay married to me any more, I would've found a way to stop.

'It's not like I didn't tell you,' he says.

'I know you did.'

'Did you think I wasn't serious about it?'

My whole body is shaking, and I don't know

what to do. Normally I'd run into Daniel's embrace as he holds me and tells me everything will be okay, but that's no longer an option. This is real, I keep telling myself with sickening heartache. I'm really losing my husband.

'Is that the end of it?' I ask. 'Can't we work on things?'

'You already "worked on things". Five minutes later, you're following Abby all over town and taking photos of her while she battles her own demons. If that's your version of fighting for us, I don't want to see what neglect looks like.'

'But I'll try. I really will!'

Daniel shakes his head and lowers it. 'I just don't believe you.'

'Please, give me until the day of my first appointment. That's all I ask.'

'That's over a week from now.'

'Exactly, so there's no hurry to get things filed. Mia doesn't have to grow up in a broken home. We don't have to spend our lives regretting our mistakes.' I go to him, desperately wrapping a hand around his forearm and then turning his face to look at me. 'Just until the first appointment. After everything we've been through, is that so much to ask?'

'Louise, I—'

'Just a few more days. If I make so much as one slip-up, I'll go to stay in a hotel and won't bother you any more. You have my word on that, as your wife. As the mother of your child. Please, just... Please.'

Daniel sighs, and suddenly, the weather means nothing. There's no more promise of long, happy summer days out in the garden. There's no decision to make on having a second child with the man of my dreams. Everything I took for granted now hangs in the balance, my entire life as I know it depending on his next words.

'Okay,' he says. 'Just a few days. No more conflict.'

I lean into him, hugging him as he weakly holds me back.

'I promise.'

THE WALK back is incredibly awkward. Daniel has given me one last chance, but it feels more obligatory than anything else. I don't know what's wrong with me because most women would make an effort to get along with Abby – to grin and bear whatever sadistic crap she throws at me – but I find my own promise was empty.

I'll risk it all to prove she's trouble.

The stakes are higher now. If I mess this up, I'll be living my life without a husband. Mia will have the worst childhood, growing up with her mother and father in separate homes. I'd need to find a job, which are very hard to come by in Dolcester. Just ask Abby. She's been failing to gain employment for days now.

Or, perhaps, pretending to seek it.

When we reach the house, I stop Daniel just outside the front door. He reaches out and wipes his thumb across my cheek, clearing the leftover tears away. It shocks me that he's not crying, even though he never was much of a crier. Then again, I can see he's truly defeated by all that's happened. For all I know, he does it in private.

'Does Abby know?' I ask. 'That you want a divorce?'

'We talk, as you might imagine, but she doesn't know I've decided.'

It hits me all over again: he's *decided*. This could very well be the end of Mr. and Mrs. Doctor Wright. I'm trying to compose myself for Mia's sake. If she's awake in there, the last thing I want is for her to see me in pain. It helps if Abby doesn't see, too.

I'd hate for her to know she's winning.

We go inside, where Abby is sitting in the kitchen with Mia in front of her, a spoon of scrambled eggs being flown into her mouth with an aeroplane imitation. She looks at Daniel as we enter, offers a look of sympathy, then – wickedly performed – does the same to me.

'Everything okay?' she asks.

'It's getting there.'

'Good.'

I pay no attention and go into the kitchen, making my way around the table to reach Mia. Abby stops me and says she's got it all under control. I want to tell her to back the hell off and get away from my daughter, but Daniel is staring at me from the other end of the kitchen. This is it, I realise. My first in a long series of hard efforts to let Abby walk all over me.

So I stand back and pretend I trust her.

As I go to the fridge for a bottle of water I like to keep in there, Abby hauls Mia out of the high chair. She giggles at first, then goes quiet. I watch as she concentrates in Abby's arms, pointing at her and moving her lips in a weird puckering motion.

I know what's happening, but there's no way to stop it. All I can do is stand there with my soul getting crushed as my daughter points at Abby and, for the first time ever, starts and finishes a word with undeniable clarity.

'Mama.'

Seven days.

That's all I have left to keep proving I'm okay – that my mental well-being is no longer threatened by Abby, and Daniel's goody-two-shoes sister is more than welcome in our house for as long as she wants. Which, it seems, is forever.

I hate that she spoke her first word to Abby, and I absolutely despise that she called her Mama. What hurt even more was that Abby laughed and shrieked with joy, kissing Mia's cheeks and remarking how proud she was. She then shared her joy with Daniel.

Neither of them so much as looked at me.

But today is a new day. What's done is done, and there's no getting around it. All I can do is focus on raising my child as best I can, keeping my mouth shut when Abby dares to corner me, smirk at me, or even slip in rude comments about how

I'm not looking my best. If you ask me, she knows all about the pending divorce and is not-so-secretly revelling every minute of it. She has it made, everything she wants falling into place.

I just don't understand *why*.

Since the moment we met, I've been nothing but nice to her. Once you take out following her and snapping some photos of her, obviously. But Abby has been the instigator in every other conflict to this day, and Daniel doesn't even see it. He's too busy figuring out if he can stand being married to me any more. And who can blame him?

Abby has designed it to look like I'm an awful person.

My luck does take a turn, however. I'm sitting in the back garden with Mia when it happens, enjoying the shade while Daniel is cooking something on the barbecue. Abby is on the sun lounger, tanning up with a paperback and my earphones plugged into her skull. Everyone is distracted, which is absolutely perfect for me.

Because they can't see my reaction to the text message from Joanna.

Can we meet? Desperate times.

I'm grinning from ear to ear, wondering who exactly Joanna is and how I can slink away. I already know Abby will jump at the chance to take Mia, so I start planning my excuse to take her with me. It takes a while to realise that this clandestine meeting might not be safe. I don't know anything about my mysterious helper, save for her name and a brief snippet of her history.

Joanna's profile is set to private.

Is that to avoid Abby or to hide something?

There's only one way I'm going to find out, and time is running scarily short. I type out my reply, telling her I'll be in the village in just a few minutes so we can finally get this dirty business over with and maybe – just maybe – expose Abby for what she truly is.

These are desperate times indeed.

And now I'm taking desperate measures.

Chapter 22
The Watcher

She sits in wait while the pub's patrons go about their day drinking and eating sandwich lunches. There's a bunch of loud men in their sixties, talking over each other outside as they discuss the football results. One person is working the bar while two people order. The tennis is on the TV, but nobody is watching. It's quiet, just how she likes it.

Nobody is aware she's carrying a knife.

It's not for Louise, who should be here any minute, but rather for Abby. The Watcher dreams of driving the blade deep into the gut of that wretched woman, and she squeezes the hilt while she dreams of it. Her sweat-slick palm greases the handle in her handbag while she imagines what it would feel like to be rid of her sister's killer once and for all.

But she's not in this to take a life. She's in it to save one. If the people of Dolcester knew what Abby Wright is capable of, they wouldn't take so much as a second glance at the difficult-to-hide knife in her pocket. But in this real world – where nobody suspects a thing – it must be tactfully concealed inside this bag.

A figure passes the window. Louise is coming, and the Watcher has been waiting for this. She doesn't know what's been going on behind closed doors, but she's been watching from afar. She saw Abby meeting a strange man – she witnessed the conversation about divorce between two otherwise happily married people while concealed among the trees.

She just doesn't know how far Abby has gone yet.

But she's about to find out.

And she'll do what's necessary.

Chapter 23
Daniel

I don't blame Louise for going out. It must be hard for her, being paranoid to the point of feeling victimised, then suddenly being told a divorce is inevitable. I know I'd certainly freak out if the shoe were on the other foot. Our marriage means everything to me.

It's just a shame it must come to an end.

I don't exactly feel in tip-top shape myself, to be honest. An outsider looking in might ask what I have to worry about – I have this incredible house with a steady career, a sister who adores me, and a beautiful daughter to call my own. The sun is shining on my perfect grass while I sizzle burger meat on an overpriced barbecue that I could easily afford. They might ask what *would* make me happy, to which my answer would be that if I could just go back to a few days ago – when Abby and Louise were about to meet for the first time and didn't hate each other yet – I could happily live in that time forever. It would truly be bliss.

But life doesn't work like that. Things happen, and other things change. Your loved ones can suddenly become strangers almost overnight, leaving you to wonder if it ever would've worked in the first place. Sometimes these changes cause misery.

Which pretty much sums up how I feel.

'Is everything okay?' Abby asks on her way to the bathroom. Mia is nearby in a large playpen full of toys that we keep in the shade. Abby looks at her to check she's not climbed out, then returns her concerned eyes to me. 'You look pretty rough.'

'I'm fine,' I say. 'Just processing what happened earlier.'

She nods because I already told her about confronting Louise with my decision on the divorce. She didn't say much about it, other than she's sorry things didn't work out. Now here she is, at my side and checking on me like the good sister she is.

'Do you need anything from me?'

'No, thanks. I'll survive.'

'I don't want you to just survive. I want you to be happy.'

'In time, I will be.'

Abby sighs and watches Mia again, who is clacking two plastic cups together. Meanwhile, I turn the sausages on the barbecue and dodge the aromatic puff of steam that hisses towards my face. It smells divine, but my appetite is long gone. So is Louise, and Abby never wanted food in the first place. I don't know why I'm still bothering.

'Why don't you take a break for the rest of the day?' Abby says.

'What about Mia?'

'I think I can handle her. How hard can it be?'

'You'd be surprised.'

'But I've fed her before, got her back to sleep, and she loves being around me.' Abby's lips curve upwards into a smile she's not even trying to hide. 'She called me Mama.'

I nod because I don't know what to say. Poor Louise had to stand by and hear that while I stupidly celebrated Mia's first word as if it wasn't heartbreaking for my wife. Am I even a good husband, I wonder? Do I really deserve someone who makes me happy?

Abby disappears to the bathroom, leaving me alone with my thoughts again. On her return, she playfully wrestles the tongs from my hand and starts to manage the food herself. I try telling her I'm more than capable, but she won't have any of it.

Apparently, I'm to have a day off, enjoying myself while my wife has wandered off and my baby is in the hands of someone else, albeit someone I trust. But it's been so long since I've had my own time I wouldn't even know what to do with myself. I don't want to stray too far from home in case I'm needed, and if I'm stagnant, then dark thoughts will creep in.

There's only one thing I really can do.

Work.

I JUST CAN'T HELP myself.

Even though Abby has been trusted with Mia, I've still got the monitor that's linked up with the camera in the nursery. It's not that I don't trust my sister, but it's so nice to watch my little angel sleep. It's not distracting me yet because there's no sign of either one of them – I can hear Mia screaming excitedly from the kitchen, as she sometimes does when she's ready to eat. It won't be long before she's down for her afternoon nap.

Then the whole house will be uncomfortably quiet.

I'm sick with worry about the future. It feels as though something monumentally disastrous is right around the corner, and that odd feeling is unshakable. I'm trying to put my head in work mode, but I just can't stop thinking about all that's happened. Not just with Louise and Abby but with interference from Joanna Heywood. If she's reached out to my wife, there's no telling what else she'll do. All I know for sure is that she won't stop there.

I should warn Abby, really. Joanna can be very explosive, especially when she still harbours a grudge for what happened to her sister. It's not that I don't blame her – I'd be angry, too, if someone hurt Abby, for instance – which is why we need to be careful. Pain can make a person do strange things. *Dangerous* things. If Joanna is even remotely capable of acting on her unbridled hatred for me and Abby, we need to remain keen-eyed and alert at all times.

The pressure is building up. My forehead is throbbing as stress threatens to burst my brain. I can't deal with these thoughts any longer, so I turn myself to more mundane tasks, like filling out the questionnaire from the divorce solicitor. They're pretty basic questions, mostly just asking for a background on me and Louise. Luckily, our past isn't too complicated – we met, fell in love, got married, had a kid, and then Louise started to behave very strangely. I know for an absolute fact that I'll be asked to elaborate on this latter comment, so I open up a blank document on my computer and start drafting a letter covering her recent activity.

Even that brings up a whole bunch of emotions, stirring the devil in me and making me realise it's quite possible that I'm starting to hate my own wife. I feel rancid, torn apart by guilt for having such unusual emotions towards a woman I once thought it was impossible to live without. But now things are so hard that I'm just done with it all. I promised Louise I'd wait until her first appointment, but it's obvious what will happen in the meantime: she'll lose control and start pointing the finger at Abby again. Which pretty much confirms it.

We *are* getting divorced.

By the time I've finished my write-up, I'm about ready to wipe my hands of the subject. I think about heading back downstairs to see Abby, but then she catches my eye on the monitor. She might not realise the camera is on because she's singing unashamedly to Mia as she tries putting her to sleep. I snicker quietly to myself and watch intently as she lays my baby down.

Then I witness it. Something I never thought was possible. The monitor comes with me as I shoot out of my chair and hurry down the hall towards the nursery, not entirely sure I can believe what I'm seeing. Louise would go crazy if she saw this because it's just another reason to hate my sister. That's the last thing we need, so although I'm on my way to investigate, I'll most definitely keep my findings to myself.

I STAND at the nursery door, badly wanting to go in and watch but forcing myself to stop. It doesn't take much to trigger Mia – sometimes something as slight as heavy breathing can pull her out of a deep sleep – so the last thing I want is to go shoving open doors.

All I can do is wait.

I'm still watching the monitor when Abby slips out of the nursery. She pulls the door to, and we're both grinning at each other like idiots, barely able to believe the phenomenal achievement of putting Mia to sleep so quickly and efficiently. This is the first time she's ever gone down without either breastfeeding or one hour of kicking and screaming. Abby seems to have managed within two minutes, her less-than-average singing voice putting Mia into a deep slumber that – judging by her open mouth and soft snoring – she'll stay in for the whole stretch.

'How on earth did you do that?' I ask, waving her away from the hall. We go into the nearest room, which is the guest bedroom. It's nice to see that Abby has made the bed and kept things tidy, respecting our home during her stay.

Abby just shrugs, trying to play it cool but failing to hide her happiness.

'We were downstairs. She rubbed her eyes and then yawned. As soon as I knew she wanted to sleep, I brought her up here. You should have seen her – she just clung to me like she trusts me fully. I've never felt anything like that before.'

'You don't think I trust you?' I jest.

'You know what I mean. It was like she looked up to me.'

'Like you're her own mother.' It feels awful to

say it out loud, as if I'm betraying Louise somehow by choosing our daughter's allegiance. But if you saw what I just saw in the nursery, you wouldn't be able to deny how special it was. 'You'll make such a good mum someday.'

Abby blushes, shuts the door, then goes to sit in the window seat, turning her attention to the clear blue sky. She's always wanted to be a mother, but things just haven't worked out that way. It's not like her prison sentence did her any favours, too – her biological clock is ticking.

I move to sit on the bed, lowering my voice but still astounded by how easy she made it look. Mia hasn't even stirred, when she normally would have already shifted positions twice by now. 'Do you think this is a one-off, or can you always do that?'

'I've no idea. It's not like this has happened for me before. Kids hate me.'

'Come on, they don't hate you.'

'Liar. Remember that time I babysat?'

I laugh out loud at the memory that hits me like a blast from the past. When we were teenagers, I had a paper round, and Abby was jealous of me making my own money. She insisted on babysitting the neighbour's kid, who was a nine-year-old bully with a BB gun. The boy's parents warned her that she could get shot – we *all* warned her – but she didn't want to listen. She insisted that she was in control and could handle a young kid.

She was so wrong. Within one hour, the parents had to come home from their date. Abby came home early that night, covered in red marks from multiple point-blank shots of the BB gun. To this day, I don't know why they didn't take that thing off the kid. Probably because they would get shot, too, I suppose.

'That was different,' I tell her. 'The boy was a nightmare.'

'True. And Mia is a golden child, so she's easier.'

'Actually, that's not true. Mia can be very hard work.' I pat the bed, beckoning her so I can at least *try* telling her things to make her feel better. She comes over, beats a pillow into shape, then sits beside me. 'She doesn't normally eat her food, but you got her eating. She doesn't usually like sleeping, but look at her now. You'll be a fantastic mum, whether you know it or not. You just have to be patient and wait for the right man.'

I don't like the way Abby is looking at me. It goes against the image of the woman I had in my mind, as if daring me to challenge her. The problem is I can't say a word. At least, I don't think I can, but my sister soon points out that's not true.

'The door is closed, Daniel. You don't have to speak like that.'

That's when I turn and confirm she's correct. It is shut, and this is the one room in the house we know for a fact has no cameras or prying eyes. Abby checks it every night, she tells me, insisting this is the one place where we can be ourselves.

'You're right,' I say, smiling because we can let our guards down for five seconds and talk as if nobody else can hear us – so we can simply be ourselves with no more sneakily phrased sentences or code words. For the first time in ages, we no longer have to act. 'So, what shall we do about Louise now that the divorce is happening?'

Abby grins at me knowingly because, as far as we know, we're the only people on earth privy to the truth. She leans in close and whispers in my ear. 'The answer to that is the same as it's always been: we stick to the plan.'

Chapter 24

Louise

I'm not actually sure what to expect when I reach the White Lion, but perspiration is starting to dampen my armpits and forehead. It's not the sun – despite how insanely hot it is today – but rather the fact I'm about to meet the only person who seems to know the truth about Abby.

Before I go in, I wait on the side of the road and take one last look at my phone. If there's anything at all that I can find online about this whole situation, I'm going to use it. I begin with Joanna's profile, checking once more to see if I can view her profile. The only thing it shows is the main photo of her – she's probably around my age, sitting on a tyre swing and looking deadpan at the camera. From the way she's not even attempting to smile, it's possible she has no sense of joy left in her life. It wouldn't be the greatest shock, seeing as she's spent the past six years mourning her sister, while Abby now roams free.

Giving up on that far too quickly, I then type her name into a search engine. There's very little about her, save for her name after giving the statement about losing a loved one. But she's hardly alone – the victim's entire family talked about how wonderful she was, all singing her praises with the knowledge that they'll never see their sister and daughter again.

It's crushing.

When I realise this is a lost cause, I close the tabs on my phone and stow it in my pocket. I take a deep breath and look up at the pub in front of me. This place is usually associated with a good time – many summer days and nights have been spent here, enjoying drinks while catching up with the locals. I think about when Daniel first came to Dolcester. Everyone made a fuss of him, which they absolutely should have, considering how handsome and wonderful he is. This was before anyone knew about his tragic past with Abby, which, in my eyes, made him all the stronger as a man. I wish I could be as composed as him.

But I'm not. My actions have led me to a very desperate place. I'm facing a divorce, and the only thing that can keep me married is whatever secret this Joanna woman has to say. I'm sceptical, of course, terrified that she just wants an excuse to get me close so she can hurt me – finally getting some revenge on Abby.

Well, if that's the case, she's doing the wrong thing. Abby despises me, and that's why I'm here: to get the dirt on the woman who's torn my life apart from the inside – to gain knowledge that I can use to win back my husband, proving once and for all that Abby is rotten to her core. When I think about how close I am to obtaining this knowledge, it hardly seems like a risk to head into a public place and meet a total stranger.

That's where I find my courage, take a deep breath.

Then head inside.

THE WOMAN I find in the pub is nothing like her photo. She's all hunched over, a broken husk of the person she used to be. Her eyes are dark hollows, the whites streamed with flecks of red. Her skin has the complexion of someone who hasn't seen daylight in years. She's completely unrecognisable, so much so that I wouldn't even know it was her if she didn't wave me over.

'You're Joanna Heywood?' I ask, standing at the end of her corner table.

She nods. 'Good to finally meet you. Want to sit down so we can talk about it?'

I'm inclined not to, feeling slightly suspicious about the way she has a hand in her bag. She must see some of the concern in my expression as she slowly pulls out the empty hand and rests it on the table with the other. Seeing no sign of danger, I join her.

'I don't know where to start,' she says, her voice somewhat croaky. 'Why don't you tell me a little about yourself and how far Abby has sunk her claws into your life?'

'With all due respect, I don't know you. You're the one who wanted to meet, so maybe you should start explaining what exactly you want from me? I assume you live in London where your sister did, so if you made it all the way up here, then what's the issue?'

Joanna nods thoughtfully, reaches for her glass, then realises it's empty. She stares at it, rocking it back and forth as the lemon slides around the melting ice cubes. I can tell she's thinking about how to phrase it, and while she does that, I glance around to make sure people are here if I need them. The pub is empty, but one of the barmen – Dave – gives me a nod to make sure I'm okay. I return the motion doubtfully, and he leans over the bar, watching but out of earshot. I love this village and everyone in it.

Except for Abby, that is.

'Abby Wright and I have a past,' Joanna says. 'It goes back before the crash. She used to hang around with my sister for a while, back in their late teens, but I never really trusted her. Anita was a fun-loving girl who easily attached herself to people even if they weren't good for her. Obviously, that would later cost her life.'

'Wait.' I lean on the table. 'She died in a car accident, didn't she?'

'Is that what she told you? That it was an accident?'

'From the very start, yes. Even in court—'

Joanna waves a hand dismissively. 'Oh, of course she lied in court. Anything to get out of what she did. The truth is, she'd been threatening her for quite some time. See, Abby always wanted a baby, and my sister... well, let's just say she wanted one, too. She used to tell all her friends about how she intended to be a mum someday, but at the time, she was seeing a guy who didn't want kids. Bright future ahead of him, all that stuff.'

'I don't understand. What does Anita wanting a baby have to do with Abby?'

'Well, Abby was jealous. She always was a malicious thing, and she couldn't conceive after a hockey accident she had a couple of years prior. So when Anita announced she'd slept with someone at a house party and had a bun in the oven, things turned sour.'

'Sour how?'

'Abby insisted she would be a better mum and that Anita should give up her kid.'

'But Anita didn't have the baby. The newspapers would have mentioned it.'

'That's because it was hush-hush. We didn't even tell our parents.'

'But the autopsy would have revealed it.'

'It didn't get that far. I talked her into having an abortion long before the crash.'

My head is starting to pound with information overload. The stranger across from me has been spinning a yarn for a couple of minutes now, but none of it pertains to me and my own predicament. I'm starting to grow a little agitated, to be honest.

'Okay,' I say. 'So your sister had an abortion. So what?'

'So, Abby saw this as some kind of aggressive act. Like it was all done to spite her. She cornered Anita a few times, slapping her around and saying that baby could have found a good home with her if only she hadn't ended the life inside her. Abby was in some kind of rage, and she was hell-bent on making my sister suffer. The last words either of us heard from her before the accident were that Anita should watch her back. Although I really shouldn't use that word – *accident*. It's very misleading.'

'You're saying she did it on purpose?'

'Would that really be so surprising?'

Not at all, I think, still struggling to take it all in. Since the moment I first met her, Abby has shown me nothing but her evil side. No matter who was sitting in front of me and explaining she was capable of murder, I wouldn't struggle to believe it. The real trouble is making Daniel believe it, and the very thought of his name brings up another issue.

'No, that can't be right,' I say. 'Daniel was there that night. He said it was an accident.'

Joanna shakes her head, then meets my eye. 'That's another thing we need to discuss.' She puts a hand on mine and hits me with another devastating fact. 'He's a liar, too.'

Now my head is spinning, and I don't know what to make of this woman any more. I was always willing to accept that Abby is a piece of work, but Daniel? He's a perfect man – the good doctor everyone sees him as. I've never had reason to suspect him of anything.

Unless...

'Daniel has been helping Abby ever since,' Joanna says. 'It was never a secret that Abby had something of a dark side. He knew it as well as anyone else. We all argued about it countless times. Shortly before the night Anita was killed, we told him that Abby had been threatening my sister. It was an absurd accusation, he said and put up a wall to defend her.'

'That sounds familiar. He's been sticking up for her since day one.'

'There you go, then.' Joanna takes a breath. 'I know he wasn't involved in the car wreck itself because as soon as we got the news, I saw him running down the street in the direction of the scene. By the time I got there, he was insisting he'd been in the car and provided a testimony that Abby had been driving safely. I was going to argue it in court, but Abby got to me before the police did, whispering in my ear that if I tell anyone the truth, then I'll die next.'

A dry lump forms in my throat. 'You believed she would kill you?'

'Why wouldn't I? She'd just killed my sister.'

'But you reached out to me. You're telling me all of this now.'

'Because I don't want you to suffer like the others.'

'What others? What are you talking about?'

Joanna pulls her hand away and starts wringing out her fingers. She lowers her gaze, only to look up again when a small group of boys in their early twenties come in making a noise. She asks if we can take it outside to get some air, which I quickly agree to because the walls are starting to close in on me, and I'm about ready to scream just to let out some tension.

Outside, we don't sit. We simply stand by the door as Joanna rests a hand on her almost non-existent stomach. 'There were others after Anita. Remember I said that Abby couldn't conceive? She made her way from friend to friend, paying special attention to those who were pregnant or had the potential to be. I've got no proof of this, but I think Daniel was helping her.'

'Why would he do that? Didn't he...?'

Joanna gawks at me, urging me to reach the conclusion on my own.

'Wait,' I say, my soul leaving my body with a chill. 'Is my baby at risk?'

'That's exactly why I'm here, Louise. Bad things happen to anyone who gets remotely close to Abby. She's a magnet for trouble, and I don't think it's a coincidence. I've been watching Daniel over the years, and the same thing always seems to happen: he meets a woman, gets her pregnant, and then leaves when the baby miscarries.'

I'm stunned, barely able to breathe. My mind drifts to Mia, making me wonder if she's safe at home. I want to run as fast as I can and check on her, but Joanna is looking at me with such halting intensity, as if to beg that I finally let the truth sink in.

'Your baby may not be *your* baby for much longer,' she says. 'I believe that while Abby has been in prison, Daniel has been preparing you to give birth to a kid they can raise together. I don't know what will happen to you, but it won't be good.'

I shake my head, not wanting to believe it. 'But why? Why would they do it together?'

'Because despite what you've been told, Daniel and Abby are not brother and sister.' Joanna fixes me with her steely eyes as she elaborates on the crushing truth about my husband and his supposed sibling. 'They're lovers, and they have been for fifteen years.'

Chapter 25
Daniel

THERE HAS BEEN a strict set of rules to get us this far.

Rule number one: Abby and I are brother and sister as far as anyone is concerned. Nobody needs to know how madly, deeply, and utterly uncontrollably we love each other. That stuff is reserved for us in our own private, intimate little moments.

Rule number two: there is no talk of the truth in any place other than her own bedroom. There are no cameras or microphones here, so as long as the door is shut, we're free to discuss things freely. While Louise is out of the house, that is.

Rule number three: the most important rule of all, because it's the only thing that keeps us safe as we plan to impregnate the victim and then take her baby for ourselves to live happily ever after somewhere abroad. That means nobody from our past can even come close to revealing the truth, so imagine my panic when Joanna reached out to Louise. I knew at the time that we didn't have much time left, which is why Abby had to work harder at making my wife look, sound, and feel like a complete nutcase.

I had my own part to play, too. Everything that happened was by our own design. Abby and I spent hours – amassing to months – figuring out the things that might make Louise question herself. And we did it, each playing our roles to perfection. Half the town knows me as the good guy, while my friends and Louise's are starting to question her sanity. That's what they'll tell the police when this all blows up – that Louise wasn't in her right mind.

Technically speaking, she's been her own enemy this whole time.

I slide out of bed, having enjoyed a long-overdue screw with Abby. How we could have destroyed the house from her loud screams as I pleasured her, knowing Louise wasn't within earshot. It's happened multiple times since her release from prison, and I can't state enough how

The Sister-in-Law

much better it is than having to keep Louise happy. Boring in life, boring in bed.

Unlike my 'sister'.

Just in case we get caught, I quickly throw my clothes back on and toss Abby's to her. She snatches them from the air and starts covering up that lovely, skinny, naked body of hers. I watch her, doing my best not to drool at the perfect woman in front of me.

I don't even pay attention to the screaming baby monitor beside me.

'Shut that thing up,' Abby says, slipping a tight top over her head. She points at the monitor, creasing up her face with annoyance when I don't move. 'Daniel, that bloody baby is making a hell of a racket. Either turn off the sound or go and shut it up.'

I hate when she refers to my baby as 'it', but she can do whatever she likes. The beautiful Abby Wright – changed legally when we were teenagers so suckers like Louise could more easily buy in to our ruse – can have anything she wants for as long as we live. Seeing as my baby is soon to be *our* baby, she can call Mia whatever she likes. It's not as if I care too much – I never was interested in having kids, but Abby demanded it, and who am I to refuse her?

I'm simply the man in her life, there to give her whatever she wants.

All I want in return is her touch.

Mia just won't quieten down, which really puts me in a position. The last thing Abby wants is to have to deal with a baby while she's trying to rest after a good bang. At times like this, I really do wonder if she will actually be a good mum. The core of a decent woman is there, but sometimes she puts her own needs before anyone else's.

Things will be different with my little girl though. Mia is an absolute delight, despite her difficulty when it comes to sleeping. She's been screaming for a while now, her shrieking growing out of control while she screams at the top of her tiny little lungs. I go to her, pick her up, and rock her as she slowly simmers down to a whimper.

Just when I think I've got it, she screams again. I love this girl, but Christ can she wind me up. It's all about her – always will be, unless we train her to understand that we won't always come running whenever she throws a fit – which can get extremely tiresome.

I try a different technique, sitting on the chair in the nursery and singing to her. Her beady little eyes light up as she claps her hands to tell me she's happy and she knows it. Her tear-soaked cheeks beg to differ, but it's fine. Whatever keeps her from deafening me and Abby all over again with that high-pitched shriek of hers.

Mia grows tired of clapping, rubs her eyes, then falls on to my chest. I rub her back and shush her, knowing I'm pretty much trapped. She doesn't like it when I put her down, and it's not like Abby wants to come and help. There is one other option, and that's to take her back into the guest bedroom so she can settle on a real bed. Providing Abby is dressed, that is.

It's probably the right thing to do. Louise will be back before we know it, and it's almost time to act – to set the events in motion so we can get rid of her once and for all. After that, Mia will belong to Abby and me as we live the rest of our lives finally having what we want.

And there's not a thing Louise can do about it.

. . .

It takes a while for Mia to fully settle, her eyes closing way too slowly. I wish she would hurry up because I'm eager to get things going. There's no telling how long Louise will be out, and if we don't clarify the plan before she gets here, then we'll have to wait even longer.

We've already waited long enough.

When Mia finally falls back asleep, I carry her gently back to the guest bedroom with her dozing in my arms. Abby pulls a disgusted face when I enter, then sits up straight and reaches out to our baby. I hand her over and let Mia's new mummy cradle her, even though Abby is clearly not in the mood for being a parent today. That's another red flag, if you ask me.

But I want Abby, and this is the only way to keep her.

'Are you ready to do it?' she asks.

'I think so. It's just the acting that's hard.'

'Meh. You'll get through it. You always do.'

She's right. Every time this has happened – all those times I've had to emergency-exit from someone's life because they've failed to deliver a healthy child – I've talked my way out of it by gaslighting the would-be mother. I should be more confident in my acting abilities. After all, I tricked Louise for four whole years, didn't I?

I go to the window where Abby stood just an hour or so ago, watching the front gate at the end of the drive. It's still closed, so I know Louise isn't home yet because that airhead always forgets to shut it after her. We're safe for a little while longer.

'Want to go over the plan one more time?' I ask.

'Not in full detail because who knows how much time we have?' Abby looks down as Mia stirs on her chest, whines a little, then falls back to sleep. Abby looks up at me again as if nothing happened. 'First of all, where do we do this?'

'I say we do it right here.'

'In this room?'

'Yeah, why not? It has everything we need in it. You still have the gloves?'

Abby nods.

'And the gun?'

'In the dresser. Under the bottom drawer.'

'Great. So, let's get our stories straight.' I close my eyes and focus on my breathing, trying to recall everything as it should be. 'Louise was always a jealous person, often going through my work computer to find evidence of me cheating. It was irrational, and I told her that, but it only made her angrier. Then, when you got out of prison, she became extremely territorial and started making up lies about you just so I would kick you out of our home.'

Abby smirks and laughs softly, Mia stirring against her bobbing chest.

'It's been tearing me up inside, so I've had to reach out to people and ask for advice on how to handle an insanely paranoid woman. Those same people have already met my lovely sister, and the police won't fact-check our relationship because we have the same surname. Even if they do figure it out, we'll be long gone by then.'

'Don't forget the framing.'

'I didn't forget. That's just the part I'm worried about, so I'd rather not—'

'She's got to hurt us, Daniel. Whether you like it or not, that part has to happen.'

'Yeah, I know.' I sigh heavily and go back to watching the front lawn. It's not as if I'm afraid of getting hurt, but I am aware of the consequences. There's a small chance I'll bleed out and not make it out of this alive – which would help sell it, admittedly – but at least Mia would have Abby. A real mother as she grows up in this awful world.

'You're starting to panic, aren't you?' Abby asks.

'A little. It's hard work. Very risky, even at the best of times.'

'But we've not failed yet. Their wombs have, but we haven't.'

'This, coming from the woman who just spent six years in prison.'

'Hey, that had its perks.'

'Such as?'

Abby looks down at Mia, then starts to slowly transfer her on to the bed. She's lying on her back now as Abby kneels in front of the dresser and removes the bottom drawer. After feeding her arm through the gap and feeling around, she pulls out a Beretta 9000 pistol. She checks the magazine and, satisfied, puts the drawer back in its place. When she comes back to me, she puts the gun in my hands. I don't like the weight of it, physically *or* proverbially.

I think about the man she met in the village on the day Louise followed her. The story Abby gave was actually true for the most part; it was her cellmate's father, she did kill herself, and Abby did meet him to give him a final message. The part we kept to ourselves was that she wasn't just there for that reason alone.

She was also procuring this gun.

'Are you comfortable using that thing?' she asks, putting a hand on my thigh.

I bat it away because we don't have time for a second round between the sheets, and besides, Mia is taking up space with her arms spread out like a set of wings. 'More than. It might be my first time using a gun, but we both know I don't have an issue with murder.'

'It might not come to that.'

'No, but if it does, I'll be ready for it.'

At long last, the gate at the end of the drive swings open. Typically, Louise doesn't shut it behind her, storming up the path towards the front door. She knows – I can tell. Somehow, she's found out all about our past and is now in a rage. I'm willing to bet it was Joanna Heywood, the meddling bitch who just won't let things go. Her sister died – who cares?

She was useless anyway.

'I guess this is it,' Abby says, kissing me hard on the lips. 'Good luck.'

'We won't need luck. We came this far on our own. This is simply the epilogue.'

I turn my attention back to Louise, who's almost out of sight as she marches to the front door. There's a weird, fizzy feeling in my stomach, and I can't work out if it's excitement or fear. I'm always nervous about these things going wrong, but there is an element of joy I get from it. In this case, it will be putting an end to Louise's moping and complaints.

Soon, she'll *really* have something to complain about.

Chapter 26
Louise

'THEY'RE LOVERS, *and they have been for fifteen years.*'

There is no way to describe the icy clutch of terror when your child is in danger. It's something you can only feel, and you know it's there when your body starts acting without you telling it to. That's what I do to Joanna, leaving her in the dust while I abandon her at the pub and sprint up the road as fast as my legs will carry me.

I'm sick the whole time, my stomach twisting in knots as a deadly blow of shame hits me. Mia is alone with them right now – with her father and his insane sister.

Not sister, I must keep telling myself.

His *lover*.

I pass villagers along the way, all stopping and staring as I dash around them. Even Lisa stands aside, her brow furrowed while I run to save my child. I want to shout to them all, explaining the truth about Daniel and Abby, but there's just no time. All I can do is keep running, sweating profusely while my shins hurt and a stitch bubbles in my stomach.

The gate bashes open as I burst through it, still failing to grasp how real this is. It feels like I'm stuck in a nightmare, wading through mud while my daughter's safety hangs in the balance. They're going to take her, I realise with a frightening thud of awareness – they're going to take my baby girl and raise her as their own.

I feel sick as I rush through the front door. I start to search the house room by room, that tight sensation in my stomach starting all over again. Sweat is dripping off me, not from the summer heat but from the pain of knowing it might be too late.

I might never see Mia again.

The downstairs is empty, leaving only the upper floor to search. Each room I go into leaves me with less hope than the last. I'm looking for signs that they might have gone, but everything in the house is how I left it, except Daniel and Abby –

Oh, God, they're lovers – are no longer chilling out in the back garden.

The final room, our bedroom, is vacant. I fall back against the wall outside, staring at the floor as my body goes numb. They're gone, I think, before remembering there is *one* more room. I've had such a mental blocker on it because I've been avoiding that room for a while now, desperate to stay out of harm's way.

Out of *Abby's* way.

I collect myself and walk slowly towards the guest bedroom. It's shut, just like it always is, but that doesn't mean there are no horrors lurking behind it. My mouth is dry as a desert, my tongue feeling like sandpaper as I gather my nerves and reach for the door handle. I have no idea what to expect when I open it, but it still shocks me to my very core when I do.

It's Daniel I see first, his demeanour so casual, as if he's been expecting me this whole time. Right at his side, clinging on to him with that sadistic grin of hers, is Abby. She has a hand against my husband's chest, making me feel sick.

But that's not the worst of it.

Mia is on the bed, sleeping soundly and unaware of the danger she's in. Heartache explodes through my chest, my breathing short as I go inside to take her into my arms, stopping as soon as the gun is pointed at my face. I freeze, unsure of what to do as I've never been in this situation before – I've never even seen a real gun until today.

It's Daniel who's holding it, a new, devilish smile appearing on his lips. He suddenly no longer looks like the loving doctor, his appearance taking on something far more sinister: a sly, vindictive man who will stop at nothing to get what he wants.

'Are you going to kill me, Daniel?'

I just about manage the words before a croak lodges in my throat. This morning, when I woke up, it was a perfectly normal day. I've gone through so many emotions since then: from learning that my husband wants a divorce, to being told he was never truly who he said he was, and then fast-forwarding to now, where he's pointing a lethal weapon at my head.

'I'll do whatever it takes,' he says coldly, like a different man.

Abby comes away from the window then. I watch her, fascinated by the casual smoothness with which she applies a pair of rubber gloves and searches for something. She seems lost, looking around before finally asking Daniel for help.

'Where's the knife?'

'Oh, that's the one thing I forgot to do.'

Abby shrugs, as if all she's done is forget to add sugar to her coffee, then disappears out the door. I'm left alone with Daniel, scared to death about what they're planning to do with the knife when she returns. Between us, Mia wiggles on the bed, huffs, then settles back to sleep. It's the hardest she's slept in her entire life. She chose this moment perfectly – I don't want her to see what's going on around her.

It would scar her for life.

'Is this really happening?' I mutter to Daniel. 'Is everything I heard true?'

'That depends on what you heard. I take it you've been speaking to Joanna?'

'Yes.'

'Then indeed, it's probably all true.'

I can barely believe it. The love of my life is not only taking everything from me, but he's doing it while looking like he doesn't have a care in the world. By the time I even find a single word to say, Abby returns with the large kitchen knife from my block. Just a couple of years ago, Daniel bought me that knife set as a gift.

Now I know why.

I flinch as Abby comes towards me, thinking she intends to stab me. Daniel aims the gun at my chest and tells me to let her work. Whatever that means. I stand still, save for the uncontrollable shaking, while Abby hands me the knife and closes my fingers around it. I'm shocked and confused, staring open-mouthed through tears as she then takes the same knife in her rubber-gloved hands and walks around the bed to Daniel's side.

'What are you going to do to me?' I ask, almost with a whimper.

'You haven't figured that out yet?' Daniel side-glances at Abby, and they both smile. It makes me feel even sicker than before – they have inside jokes that I'm not privy to. Like a real couple. As if my own marriage never existed. 'It's pretty straightforward, really. First, you'll punch Abby into the mirror, giving her a black eye. Then you'll reach for the knife that you had on you all this time and stab me in the leg. All because I'm trying to get our baby to safety while you finally snap and take it out on us.'

Abby looks around at the mirror, then goes to stand by it, knife in hand. Daniel stays looking at me, piercing me with those dark brown eyes. As I stare into them, I finally understand what's happening. Just like Joanna said, they're going to take Mia away. And in order to do that, they'll need to make me look crazy.

'That's right,' Daniel says, registering the understanding in my eyes. 'You've spent a lot of time letting everyone know how paranoid you are. Don't worry, I've been doing the rounds, too. There's not a single person in this village who would believe your side of the story. Except Joanna, of course, but even she has a reputation. You know why?'

I don't ask because I'm too scared to hear the answer.

It comes anyway.

'Because we're smarter than she is. Smarter than *you* are. See, all it ever took was to push you in the right direction. You did the rest yourself. All the while, I introduced everyone around town to Abby, and every one of them thinks she's as wonderful as she really is.'

'But she's not,' I say with trembling vocals. 'She's mental.'

'That's not how the police will see it. Even with her record.'

'Wrong. Remember, you've been meeting with Joanna. Conspiring against us.'

'They'll never...'

I understand it then. Everything I've done is working against me. Not just complaining about Abby to the other villagers but even having communication with Joanna. No wonder she wanted to meet face to face – she always knew how clever Daniel was.

But that's not the worst of it. Daniel starts to laugh as it occurs to me that I have a psychiatric assessment with a professional next week. One of his suggestions, if you can call it that after he manipulated me into doing it by threatening our marriage.

If I weren't so heartbroken, I would probably be impressed.

'Anyway, that's enough out of you.' Daniel lowers the gun just a little as he turns back to Abby. Then he kisses her on the lips, my stomach doing cartwheels as my face scrunches up at the disturbing sight. It's still hard not to see them as brother and sister, but if anything will change that, it will be the passion in their kiss. 'Are you ready, sweetheart?'

'Ready,' she says.

With that, he draws back his elbow and smacks her right in the face. Abby's head snaps back as blood instantly pours from her nose. She half pushes, half falls back into the mirror, which shatters against her spine as she loses her footing. Mia screams as she wakes, while Abby stares up at me from her knees. Blood streams through her crazed smile.

I make a move for Mia, but Daniel snaps around and points the gun at me all over again. I stop dead in my tracks, fighting the urge to help my daughter – to grab her and run far, far away from this place. Meanwhile, Daniel helps Abby to her feet.

Something tells me they're not done.

I have an idea what's coming next, but that doesn't make it any less shocking.

They both move to just a few feet away from the mirror, and then she holds the knife tight in her hand. It suddenly makes sense why she's wearing gloves – my fingerprints are all over it, further backing up their coming description of tonight's events. As far as the police will know – as much as their official statements will say – it was me.

I was the one who did all of this.

Daniel checks on Abby, tilting her head back to study her nose and using his thumbs to spread her lips and check her gums. It's a more intimate version of what he's been doing every day, working as a doctor in this godforsaken village that was supposed to be a dream town. Now, even if I make it out of here as a free woman, all it will ever do is remind me of this.

Of the psychotic actions of my husband and his lover.

'That's going to heal,' he says. 'How's your back?'

'It hurts,' Abby tells him. 'But I'll be fine.'

He moves to kiss her again, but she pushes him back. Mia is still wailing, the madness in the room probably sinking into her brain as trauma. I wonder what kind of effect this will have on her as she gets older. Will she remember it, even subconsciously?

I hope not.

Abby steps forward, the knife pointing towards him. Daniel takes a deep, steadying breath while my hand cups my mouth. I can barely believe what I'm seeing, the shock of it all finally settling in while my heart bleeds for my crying daughter. I wonder how she'll turn out after all this – if she's inherited her father's psychosis.

'Are you ready for this?' Abby asks.

'Ready as I'll ever be.'

Daniel closes his eyes and stands up straight,

exposing his body to the knife. I watch in horror, telling myself not to but unable to help it, as Abby takes the knife that's covered in my fingerprints and pulls back her arm to reach a good jabbing distance.

Then plunges it into his leg.

Chapter 27
Daniel

Getting stabbed doesn't feel like you'd imagine. There's no sharp bite of pain. No burning sensation as your skin is pierced. I can now tell you from personal experience that at first, you feel absolutely nothing. The leg immediately goes numb. What follows is a strange, cold sensation, as if an ice cube has been rubbed over the thigh right before the area has been jabbed.

But I do scream. Of course I do, because a foreign object has entered my body. Mia starts up again, yelling with me as my leg feels like it's been thumped. The real pain comes when the blade is ripped out, the serrated edge tearing at my skin. That's when I grasp at the wound, blood seeping through my fingers as Abby stands back with a smile.

'Christ,' I spit through clenched teeth.

'Are you okay?' She laughs just as Louise gasps from across the room.

'No, I'm not bloody okay.'

'Can I do something?'

'Yeah, you can put the knife down.'

Abby doesn't listen because she's still laughing. This is exactly how we designed it – a wound to the leg, the same scarlet colour as Abby's nose and upper lip. It's how Louise tried to fight us off, we'll say when the police arrive. The police that *we* will call. Anything to sell the authenticity of our struggle. Anything to gain full custody of Mia.

'You two are out of your minds,' Louise says, looking pale and frail. I can tell she wants to tend to our screaming one-year-old, but I warn her not to with my eyes. She seems to accept it, backing off as she barely resembles the woman I married any more. Then again, my leg is already starting to throb, so I'm seeing through watery eyes. Her hair is a mess of brown, her eyes bloodshot. It actually makes me feel a little sick that I used to go to bed with her, having to close my eyes every time and think of Abby – only Abby, my dear, sweet lady.

'You're in no position to judge,' I tell Louise. 'Not after slowly going insane.'

'Do you think they'll believe you?' she asks.

'They'll have to. The proof is all there.'

'Speaking of which.' Abby stomps forward and slashes with the knife. I raise my arm, a heavy cut ripping across my wrist. I stumble back in shock, while Abby just stands there with a nonplussed expression. 'What? We have to really sell this. The fact you raised your arm in defence only makes it look more genuine.'

I shake my head and sigh, clutching my arm as a red stream trickles down to my hand. This has already become far messier than it had to, but it's not like we can't recover. I stand up straight, ready to finish our plan, but my head suddenly goes all fuzzy. It's not the sight of blood that bothers me, but the sight of *my* blood has always freaked me out.

'Daniel?' Abby says, calling over the sound of our crying baby. 'You okay, babe?'

'I'm...' Fine, I want to tell her, but the words barely leave my lips. I reach out for the bed as my wounded leg gives out on me, making me stumble. Then I look up at Louise, who I expect to be loving the fact I can barely stand. Abby puts a bloody hand on my shoulder as I get all light-headed. What I need is some sugar, but what I get is a drunk feeling. It's not just a sobering perspective of these events that clarifies my groggy mind, but I'm suddenly overwhelmed by a flood of memories from a life long ago. Before Louise. Before Mia.

Back when my life was different.

I MET her when I was nine. She was the girl next door, but not in the typical sense. Remember, she was only five at the time, and our parents forced us to play together. We spent a lot of hot summer days in the garden, Abby ascending the climbing frame while I sat there in the shade, playing with my Game Boy and refusing to participate in what I thought was childish.

The irony went way over my head.

She joined my school and was glued to my hip every break time. I had better things to be doing by then, already looking at secondary school and slowly swapping the games for books. We had a career day right before leaving, and they forced us to decide then and there what we wanted to do for the rest of our lives. Pretty sick when I look back on it.

The problem was I didn't know. There was nothing out in the world that attracted me. I was always good with my hands but had no interest in carpentry or using tools of any kind. I studied a lot because I found it so easy, quickly skimming through half a textbook before bed and actually taking it all in. I was no genius, but this stuff just kind of registered with me.

On my final day of primary school, as I was heading out the front gates, I saw Abby sitting on the kerb and crying. Every part of me wanted to just go home, but there was a sense of duty lurking in me. When I checked on her, she explained she'd fallen over as blood seeped from her knee. I didn't have to think about it much – I slipped off the school jumper I'd never need again, tied it tight around the knee, then gave her a piggyback home while her hot tears dripped on to the back of my neck.

When we finally got home, dropping her off on her front doorstep and making sure she'd be okay, she kissed me on the cheek and said I was her best friend in the world, then went inside. I remember standing there, completely amazed at how kind a little girl could be, even though I'd neglected her all year. If performing a single kind act was enough to make people like me, imagine what a lifetime of it would do.

I decided then and there I'd grow up to be a doctor.

The years flew by. Abby and I kept missing each other because by the time she got to secondary school, I was at college. When she came to college, I was at uni. We passed every now and then, growing more familiar and friendly each time, but we rarely spent more than a few minutes together. It wasn't until one night in a nightclub that I *really* noticed her.

She'd grown up, developed breasts, and dressed provocatively. She hugged me when she saw me, holding me tight and squeezing our bodies together. I knew instantly that she was physically attracted to me, and given that I'd had a few drinks and she was now of legal age, we spent that night together before I went back to university.

That was the end of our friendship and the start of our romance.

Abby didn't go to uni, but we made it work. I spent every spare minute with her that I could, holding her hand through traumatic experiences like her parents passing away and taking an accidental swing to the stomach from a hockey stick that rendered her barren. She confessed to me in bed one night that all she'd ever wanted was to be a mum, and now that had been taken away from her. I'd never seen a person cry like that. I still haven't to this day.

We began to drift over time, eventually breaking up for one long winter. I filled my time by keeping my head down and studying hard to become a doctor. By the time I graduated, Abby was still at the forefront of my mind. I moved back home to London so I could be close to her, only to find that her best friend – who I had never met because she was one of those *new* best friends – had drowned while swimming in a lake. Abby had been there at the time, apparently trying to save her but failing and now having to live with that failure.

But I saw the truth.

Abby was a terrible actress. She couldn't even maintain eye contact while she told me this story, and I didn't want to be lied to. I told her then and there that I'd be there for her no matter what, as long as she started telling me the truth. Eventually, she broke down and confessed that she'd held her friend's head underwater because Abby was jealous of her pregnancy. She'd killed a woman and the life inside her on that day.

And all I felt was sympathy for Abby.

For some time then, she began clinging to those who were pregnant. I saw this was a pattern but kept my mouth shut and went along with it, tagging along to dinners and occasionally acting as a taxi driver to get them to appointments. People always appreciated me when I helped a pregnant woman, except for Abby. She was jealous – I could read it in her eyes. I also noticed how she talked to these women, making them feel as though they were unfit to raise a child. It worked, too, because those women then went on to have abortions, right before something sinister befell them. When I stopped and asked Abby outright if she had anything to do with that, she always smiled and simply told me.

Yes, she had killed again.

Maybe there's something wrong with me, but I kind of understood why she did it. Envy is a powerful emotion, capable of destroying anything long-standing. I started to help her, burying her lies and acting as an alibi. Before I knew it, we were out there actively seeking pregnant women and implementing a long-term plan to harvest that baby from them. Apparently, adoption by legal means would take too long. We didn't know at the time it would be years before we finally had a chance at keeping a kid.

By the time I realised how sick this all was, I was in too deep. Abby would shun me if I started to lose interest or if I wouldn't help. She would run off with another man and tell me it was my fault for not being there for her. I believed it, too, and began acting accordingly. I started following her every command, desperate not to lose the affections of the only woman who'd ever loved me. Over time, this became a habit – a part of me that would never leave – and no matter who might grow to love me in the years to come, something had changed.

All I wanted was Abby, and I would do anything to keep her.

I FEEL her hand on my shoulder as she asks if I'm okay. I shake off the flashback, noticing right away that the baby has stopped crying. It's a relief as my head is pounding, a sickening feeling rising up to my throat. I'm pulling myself together slowly as

Abby kneels in front of me and puts her forehead against mine. She closes her eyes.

'I'm sorry I had to hurt you,' she says.

'It's okay. Do whatever you must to become a mother.'

'Oh, I will. Don't you worry about that.'

She kisses me on the lips and then stands up. I take her reaching hand and pull myself up, trying not to put too much of my weight on her. I'm ready to face Louise – to complete our plan and take Mia from her forever – but Abby sprints out of the door before I can even see clearly.

It takes me a while to understand what's happened. Mia hasn't stopped crying at all – I can faintly hear her screaming from another room. From *downstairs*. My head spins to look at the bed, seeing for myself that our baby is gone. Louise is gone, too, having made use of our intimate moment to sneak out of the room. I've never felt desperation quite like this. Abby will kill me or leave me if we fail again, making me live without her either way.

What kind of life would that be?

Shaking off the dizzy sensation that's making the room spin, I chase after Abby to help get our baby back. If Louise is still in this house, we might need to escalate our game. We can tell the police it was self-defence and never have to worry about losing Mia again.

She will be ours then, and Louise would be helpless to stop us.

We just need to stop her from leaving.

Chapter 28
Louise

It's the dumbest thing I've ever done, but I guess you can say my fight or flight reflex kicked in. It's obviously flight, as the last thing I want to do is subject Mia to these two maniacs. While they're busy hitting and cutting each other, I see a golden opportunity to grab my daughter from the bed. It's the most terrifying thing I've ever done, my palms so sweaty as I lean on to the creaky mattress, pick her up, and then run for my life.

For *our* lives.

At first, it feels like I got away with it. There are no footsteps banging down the stairs, no screams telling me to stop or die – nothing except me and my baby heading clumsily down the stairs as we rush towards the exit.

But the front door is locked.

Abby must have done it when she came downstairs to grab the knife. I start to pull off the chain, my shaky hands fumbling for the latch that I can't quite get undone. I hear it then: the footsteps thumping along the floorboards, the screams shortly following. My heart is racing as I crane my neck to see Abby leaping down the stairs two steps at a time. Mia makes an unusual sound in my arms, quite possibly her first-ever cry of true pain. I'm squeezing too hard, clinging too tightly as I try and fail to get the front door open to liberation.

There's no getting through it.

I give up and dart into the kitchen, leading Abby around the table as I go for the back door. I have no idea how far behind me she is or even *if* she's still chasing me, and looking back now might cause me to trip and fall. So I run, Mia bobbing up and down in my arms as I exit the kitchen, dash down the narrow passageway, and then arrive at the back door.

That's when Daniel leaps out, stumbling on his one good leg while the other hangs lazily beside it. He has the gun in his hand and presses the other against the door, fixing me with that evil sneer.

He's got me, it says – there's no way out of here, and it's two against one.

Heat rises to my cheeks, sweat sticking my shirt to my body. I turn on the spot, heading back through the kitchen and reversing the route I just took. Only I can't go on because Abby is standing there with the knife still in her blood-soaked fist.

I'm cornered. There's no escape. All I can do is cling to Mia as I back away from my attackers. My backside hits the cutlery drawer, and in a final, pathetic attempt at defence, I pull it open to pick out a knife.

Abby's hand clamps it shut, and suddenly, she's right in front of me. I back into the corner, seeing a small gap beside the table where I could have run through if only I acted sooner. But now Daniel occupies the exit, trapping me in the corner between the two.

I try not to cry as I hug Mia to my chest and close my eyes, wishing this was just some awful dream I could wake up from – as though when I open them, Abby will be gone, and it will just be me and my husband, living a happy, healthy life with our daughter. But I know it's not true because there's only one way this is going to end.

The Sister-in-Law

They're going to take my baby girl away from me.

Mia wriggles and writhes in my arms, jerking a finger at Abby while beaming a big, toothy grin. She doesn't understand what's happening – she doesn't know she's about to be taken away and raised as Abby's daughter. She's too young to remember me in the coming years, and if she ever finds out the truth, there won't be so much as a single memory of me. All those times we played and laughed. All those times we clung to each other lovingly through the night.

It will all be gone.

'Give me the baby and this will all go a lot smoother,' Abby says.

'Don't be stupid, Louise.' Daniel steps closer. 'You know you can't win this.'

'Hand her over.' Abby steps even closer. 'Or die like the others.'

The tears are coming. There's no way to stop them. I always wanted to be a mum. I spent years praying for this to happen, months obsessing over the baby's health when I was pregnant. A deep, unbreakable bond is about to be... well, broken.

'I can't just give her to you,' I say, shaking my head.

'Then we'll have to take her from you. Someone could get hurt.'

There's no doubting what Daniel says. I don't want Mia getting caught in the middle of a wrestle, so I do the worst imaginable thing a mother can do. It's not my proudest moment, but I simply weaken my grip on Mia.

Then let Abby take her from me.

My heart is breaking as Mia goes to her, giggling and kicking her legs excitedly. My cheeks are damp with warm tears as she backs away, taking my baby to the doorway and bouncing her around as if she's just adopted Mia. Meanwhile, Daniel stands there shaking his head, as though I'm the one who's just committed a sinister crime.

It's not until he steps into the ray of light shining through the kitchen window that another tragedy strikes me. I've been so preoccupied with keeping Mia safe that I've barely registered I'm losing a husband. It hasn't truly sunk in yet because the man standing before me only physically resembles the man I married. The loving gaze is gone. The tender touch is a thing of the past. The warm, gentle man I vowed to spend the rest of my life with is as good as dead.

The one standing in front of me is a nightmare.

'You're looking at me like you didn't see this coming,' he says. 'You can't seriously believe, after all this time, that we were so good together. Didn't it strike you as strange that we've never had an argument? Did you even stop to think about how perfect your life was, or did you just plod along like the clown you are, thinking the world simply fell into place around you? Come on, you must have known it was too good to be true?'

I shake my head, trying not to look him in the eye because it might break me. I lower my gaze to his leg, where blood is running down his knee and dripping on to his shoe. It mesmerises me, partly because I can't stand to look across the room and see my only child leave my life.

'No,' I confess. 'I thought it was love. That was how it felt.'

'Pitiful. Brunettes just aren't for me.'

'It's true, isn't it?' I ask. 'You killed the other mums. Even Anita.'

'They had it coming. One baby is all we wanted. Is that so much to ask?'

I say nothing because there are no appropriate words.

'Abby?' Daniel calls over his shoulder.

'Yes, my love?'

'Take Mia and do the finishing touches to the house, then wait in the car.'

My stomach seems to drop, a pathetic, teary gasp passing my lips. I cover it with a hand, wanting to be anywhere but here – somewhere warm and safe and comfortable with my little girl lying in my arms. I watch her from across the room, my life shattering around me as Abby waves goodbye and then leaves.

'Wait!' I yell because I can't possibly stand this any longer.

To my surprise, Abby appears in the doorway again. Mia looks at her father and pulls a funny face, like she's so excited to see him and can't wait to play. It's the most attention she's ever paid him, and now it's obvious why – he was never really interested in her.

All he wanted was Abby.

'Can I please just say goodbye to her? Let me hold her.'

'Not a chance,' Abby says, then turns to leave again.

'Wait.' Daniel goes to her, taking Mia from her arms while she stares.

'You can't be serious. She—'

'Can't do anything about it,' Daniel finishes. 'If we're going to report this woman for being violent and unfit as a mother, the very least we can do is let her say a few words of goodbye. It's not like she can run from us, is it?'

Abby shakes her head and whines like a petulant child while Daniel puts Mia in my arms for just one minute. How am I supposed to fit a lifetime into sixty seconds? What can I possibly say to make any of this okay?

'The clock's ticking,' Daniel says. 'Say what you need to say, woman.'

Still shaking like a leaf, I wipe the tears from my face and look my daughter in the eye. She grins up at me, reaching out to touch my face. I let her do it, sniffle, and try to compose myself, then talk to her straight from the heart.

Mia won't remember any of this. It's more for me. If I'm supposed to go the rest of my life without my own daughter, my last words to her should be something poetic and magical. I never was one for poetry, and corny speeches aren't quite my cup of tea, but when her eyes meet mine, it's just like the first time we met. The words come easily then.

'You're the best thing that ever happened to me.' My fingers caress her baby-soft cheek. Mia giggles. 'Even when things were at their hardest – through the teething and the long nights – you always meant more to me than anything in the world. Mummy has to go away now, but whatever happens, I want you to know that my life is incomplete without you.'

'Yuk,' Abby says.

Daniel smiles at her, then resumes his watch over me.

There are no other words. No dragging it out by filling the silence with messages that mean nothing. All I can do is hold her close, Mia resting her head on my shoulder as I embrace her for the last time. I take a deep breath, closing my eyes and smelling her. I take in every sensation – her weight in my arms, the slight adjustment of her feet as she tries to get comfortable. I want to remember this moment for the rest of my life because wherever I'm going next, this is the one memory that will keep me warm at night.

'I love you, little girl.'

That's the end of it. My heart breaks all over

again as Daniel takes her from my arms. To make matters even worse, Mia is blissfully unaware of our separation. She kicks around with joy as Daniel pulls her to his own chest. He looks down his nose at me then, as if I'm some kind of filth he just stepped in. I never thought I'd see that look from him.

'Just so we're clear,' he says, 'you've been slowly losing your mind for some time. I've made plenty of hints around the village that you're becoming difficult – changing for the worse. I caught you trying to beat up Abby, punching her in the face and sending her into that mirror. When I tried to stop you, it turned out you had a knife. You stabbed me, and you're going to get locked up for that. You then tried again, swiping at my chest. That won't help your case. You'll be unwell – too mentally unstable to raise a child. But don't worry, because as soon as you're behind bars, Abby and I will take good care of her.'

'I'll find you,' I mutter.

'Good luck with that. We'll go abroad, change our names, live together as lovers.'

I think it's bile that I taste in my throat, but I'll never know for sure. My attention is stolen by the look on Mia's face – that happy, lovable young girl who's going to grow up to be so smart and brave and maybe change the world. Is that how it will happen, or will the psychopaths raising her turn her into something wicked? Something violent.

Someone like them.

I bite back the foul taste and watch my daughter as she's carried towards the door. It's all I can do not to cry, fighting the urge to run forward and make one last attempt to claim her back. But I know what will happen: Abby is standing nearby, the bloodied knife on the worktop beside her as she narrows her eyes at me, just waiting for an excuse. *Hoping* she can finish me off. She would do it, too, because I think she always wanted that.

She always wanted me dead.

Chapter 29
Daniel

It's almost time to take off the rubber gloves.

The house just needs a few more splashes of detail. I set to changing those things myself, taking Mia on a tour of the ground floor while knocking chairs over and smashing framed family photos off the walls. It makes her chuckle, and that squeaky little laugh would make my heart melt if I had room in it for someone other than Abby.

Speaking of which, I return to her in the kitchen. She's gone back inside, standing so close to Louise that it looks like they're about to engage in a fight to the death. It's not like Louise would ever dare fight back – she's a pathetic coward and always has been – but Abby has never held back on telling me how much hate she feels for my wife. It's funny – she used to say she got so used to playing the part of angry psycho she actually started to *feel* that disdain. Almost like she's Daniel Day-Lewis, method acting and finding himself in too deep.

'Don't knock her around too much,' I tell her, worrying that it might throw a spanner in the works when it comes to selling our story to the police. 'And wait until we're ready to go, then put the final bruises on her. Any marks need to look fresh.'

'Stop teasing me.' Abby grins.

I don't necessarily trust her alone in a room with Louise, but there's no other choice. Before we can get out of here, I need to find my phone and put up the finishing touches. To do that, I put Mia down in the nursery cot and then start scratching wallpaper along the hallway. My phone is on the bed, smeared in blood by the time I start putting my filthy hands all over it. This will be vital to the plan – the police *must* be called when we leave.

By the time I've made the upstairs look a mess, I take one last glance at our bedroom. Our marital bed is a mess of duvet and sheets, surrounded by furniture that's been tipped over. It was Louise's rage, I'll tell the police. She went mad and started tearing things apart. A small laugh escapes me, and then I pick up her perfume from beside me on the floor. It was always my favourite – a sweet, summery scent that actually helped entice me into bed with my dear wife. I spray it into the air and sniff the mist that rains over my face, enjoying it one last time.

Next time I enter this room, it will be to clear up and sell the house.

Finally, I go into the nursery and take Mia from the cot. For one more additional effect, I use my heel to kick in the bars. The frail wood snaps too easily, the wooden poles looking like mangled teeth. It's another thing that will help with authenticity – Louise is so insane that even Mia isn't safe. Look what she almost did, I'll say, pointing at the wrecked wood.

This is it, then.

The final goodbye.

I take one last look at the upper rooms, kiss Mia on the cheek, and then head downstairs to start my new life. One where Louise isn't even remotely in the picture, where Abby and I can raise this little bundle of joy as an item, becoming parents at long last.

Together.

. . .

I FIND Abby in the kitchen, even closer to Louise than she was before. Louise is backed up against the worktop, her eyes wide as she leans back as far as she can get from Abby. It should upset me to see my own wife looking like that, but I lost all sympathy for her while getting caught up in the act. Kind of like Abby, I guess. And... you know, Daniel Day-Lewis.

'It's time,' I tell her.

The sun shifts, illuminating Abby's delicate features as she turns around to give me the nod. Louise's red, tear-filled eyes follow Mia as she slinks in the middle. This is what a defeated woman looks like, I suppose. Frozen, helpless, and broken.

I let out a short, humoured huff and then give Abby the final nod. With that, she hurls the knife across the room, rips off her rubber gloves, then stuffs them into her pocket. She then draws back her arm and delivers a slap so hard that we probably could have heard it from the next room. I shield Mia's eyes, hiding the truth from her about just how dark this messed-up world can be. It's as if she didn't see Abby stab me – like she didn't scream when I put her new mummy through a mirror. Stuff she'll forget in time, I'm sure.

I just hope the damage isn't already done.

Louise starts sobbing audibly now. It pains me to hear it just because of how brutal it is. I'm not nearly sorry enough to make it stop – this is, and always has been, the plan – but that doesn't mean I have to stick around and watch.

'I'm going to get things going,' I say. 'Stop when she starts to look dizzy.'

'Take the fun out of it, why don't you.' Abby turns just enough for me to see her sneer. Her teeth disappear behind her lips when she sees the look on my face, which tells her how deadly serious I am. 'You're joking, right?'

'No. It needs to look realistic. Like you've been in a fight.'

'For crying out loud.' Abby sighs. Then: 'Fine.'

It's probably not the safest thing to do, but I leave them alone together for good, taking one last look at my wife. Next time I see her will probably be in court as we fight for custody over Mia. This precious little baby of mine is watching the door as we head towards it, not giving her real mother so much as a glance. It makes me surprisingly happy because, from this moment on, we can begin our lives as a brand-new family.

The hot summer sun attacks us the moment we

get outside. Mia buries her face in my chest to get away from it, but there's little I can do. With her in my arms, I open the garage and unlock the Jaguar. Mia doesn't put up much of a fight – similar to her ridiculous mother in that regard – seemingly grateful for the shade as I struggle to strap her into the car seat and wipe the blood from my dirty hands off her cheeks. It only clears a little, smearing the rest.

When she's in, I close the door and take a moment to breathe. All the stress has been building up over the past few days, and I just want one minute alone before we're all over the news, putting up another front to hide the truth. The real acting is about to begin.

But I can hear Abby screaming. The words are unclear, but she's letting out her rage as she usually does before saying goodbye to a victim. I put my bloody hands in my pockets and lean against the driver-side door, waiting for the yelling and the smashing of wood – the dining room table, perhaps – to reach its inevitable end.

When I'm left in silence, I decide it's finally time.

I take the phone from my pocket and call 999. There's an immediate answer as I start running

The Sister-in-Law

around the car to sound out of breath. It sounds genuine enough for my liking, even if the words do come out a little stiff.

'You've got to help me. She's going crazy in there.'

'Sir, please relax,' the woman says, falling for it easily. 'What's the situation?'

'My wife has stabbed me. She's hurting my sister. Our baby is... Oh, God.'

The rest of the call is a mess of panicked speech, but I use the important keywords; insane, violent, dangerous. I end it by saying I have to get out of here. I don't wait to hear if the police are on their way, simply hanging up and grinning. It was the perfect performance, I think as I open the car door and start to get in.

That's when *she* stops me.

She's standing in front of the car, a ghost from the past coming back to haunt me. Red-hot fury explodes within me, and I can't decide whether to shoot her with the gun in my pocket or get in the car and run her down. Because time is so short, I opt for the former, reaching for the Beretta and pointing it right at her as I take steps in her direction.

But she's smiling.

'Do you want to die, bitch?' All I want from her is one last tear before I finish her off. Joanna has been a thorn in my side for far too long, always just one step behind me while I try to fix myself into a new victim's life. It's her fault we've had to wait so long – her fault we were almost caught this time, having to move on and start afresh all over again.

Then I see it. The reason for her smile.

It's not just her standing on the drive. The police are here, too, but they're not here to *save* me. They're here to *arrest* me for my crimes. And if they ever needed even the slightest touch of proof that I'm secretly a very dangerous man, this is it.

Because I'm still holding the gun when they rush me.

THE MORE TIME PASSES, the more people I see.

It's not just Joanna, and not just the police, but that wicked piece of work has brought most of the village to view my demise. I feel like a goldfish in a bowl, a glass wall separating me from the rest of society as the policemen tackle me. Blurred images of their shocked faces whizz through my mind while I fall, struggling against the strength of the three officers who once came to our gender-reveal party. Two of them were at our wedding, watching us exchange meaningless vows with dopey looks on their faces.

'Thought you could get away with it again, didn't you?' Joanna asks, smirking.

'Go to hell,' I say as I'm forced on to my front. The cold, hard ground presses against my cheek as I'm powerless to stop it. 'Maybe your whore sister has saved you a seat.'

What really hurts is that her smile doesn't fade. She knows she's won, and everything I've ever worked towards is completely down the drain. All I can think about now is Abby and what's happening inside. Has she roughed up Louise enough? Is there a version of this where she might get away with it? If we're lucky, perhaps I could spend some time behind bars while she goes out and starts working on the next victim. She deserves that.

She deserves happiness.

The villagers are filling up my front lawn and driveway. Some are taking photographs and videos with their phones, which they'll undoubtedly share on social media. This is the end for me – I just know it is. Mia, who I'll never get to hold again, is soundless in the back of the Jaguar that I'll never get to drive again.

At least, that's what they think.

I'll serve my time and get out. *Eventually*. It might take five, ten, or fifteen years, but when the day for my liberation finally comes, I'll find Louise and take it all out on her. I'll reclaim my child no matter how old she is. Until then, I'll just have to sit patiently in a prison cell and think back to this moment – to the shame and disgrace I feel as the villagers watch the end of my life as I know it. Meanwhile, Joanna disregards the policeman's order and runs into the house to stop Abby from doing what she always wanted to do.

To kill Louise, as a token of her hate.

Chapter 30
The Watcher

THE WATCHER IS NO LONGER a watcher. She is merely Joanna Heywood, the sister of Daniel's victim. Of *Abby's* victim from long ago. Things were different back then because she was clueless – she knew the mentally unstable couple were involved in Anita's death, but proving it was somewhat harder. She had to wait, bide her time while longing for the perfect moment.

That day is today.

The knife she carried is gone – thrown into the river right before she called the police because she couldn't trust herself not to use it. Louise was no longer in sight by then, but Joanna screamed the truth as loud as she could while running through the village towards the house. People didn't understand at first, but then word started to spread. Now, here she is, with the more talkative side of Dolcester seeing Daniel's true face for themselves while she runs inside.

Abby has her hands on Louise's throat when she comes in. Joanna doesn't stop to think because in her eyes, that might as well be her sister. She lunges forward with years of hate and fury, knocking Abby over with her full weight and momentum.

'You!' Abby yells as she hits the floor.

But it's too late for her now. Joanna is already on top of her, delivering one hard slap to end them all. Abby's cheek turns bright pink, and she gives in almost immediately. Joanna, meanwhile, cranes her neck to see Louise just standing there, afraid and broken.

'Go,' Joanna says. 'Be with your baby, and never look back.'

A couple of the villagers come in then, followed by more police. Joanna is pulled away from the woman who killed her sister. It's not the end she wants – what she really wanted to do was use the knife she's been keeping for so long – but this will have to suffice. Whether she manages to end Abby's life or not, at least the dirty work is done.

Abby Wright is in custody, and Anita Heywood can rest in peace.

Chapter 31
Louise

Only two months have passed, and life is already completely different.

For starters, we're officially moving out of the house today. I can't wait to live somewhere where I'm not haunted by the memories of that horrific day. Mia and I are going back to London, where we'll start a new life by initially living off the funds I've been squirrelling away for four years. Daniel always jokingly called it 'pocket money' without realising it rarely touched my pocket. Maybe, deep down, I knew something bad would happen.

Or maybe I was just being careful.

The boxes are all packed and loaded on to three different removal lorries. One of those is mine, carrying everything Mia and I will need for our fresh start. The other two are Daniel's possessions. I've paid the drivers an additional hundred pounds each to say that if the contents of their vehicles were stolen overnight, I wouldn't file a complaint. I think they understood.

I never want to see my husband's crap again.

When the lorries are gone, it's just me and Mia standing on the front doorstep with a used car sitting nearby. It's not much – a good-condition Ford Mondeo in my daughter's favourite shade of green. We got it for a steal, but it's not like we had to pay. All of our money comes from my half of the house we just sold. It's funny how things work out.

I look up at the house, with Mia in my arms. She's getting heavier, putting a strain on my back and making me sweat. The late-September breeze is refreshing though, and I love the rain-like smell that settles into the drive's gravel as yellowing leaves rustle across it. I'm trying to decide if I'll miss this place – if there's even a small part of me that will think back to my years with Daniel. There will be *some* things. Like how good he was with Mia and how fun he could be behind closed doors, once he dropped the 'good doctor' act. But those things are gone now, living on only as memories I intend to forget.

Even Mia won't remember.

I hear footsteps come up behind me, accompanied by a dragging sound. I turn, and Mia points at the women with the adorable sound she often makes when curious about something. Lisa is standing there with a Victoria sponge in her hands, telling me she made it as a goodbye gift. I thank her, give her a loose and awkward hug, then say goodbye forever as she puts it on the roof of the car and then vanishes from my life. I'd like to say I'll miss her, but the truth is I don't think I'll miss anything to do with this life. I just want it behind me.

When Lisa is gone, we're left alone with Joanna. She's put on a little weight in the past two months. That's down to the wonder of eating well and not touching a beer in six weeks. We've become friends over time, which started when I let her temporarily move in with me so she could avoid going home. She was losing her flat and wanted out anyway. Given how good she's been with Mia ever since, we've discussed her coming with us back to London. She'll be near family then, and in the meantime? I'd be happy to have her as a nanny.

It's not like we can't afford it.

'Are you ready to go?' she asks, pushing down the handle on her suitcase.

I nod, and she loads the car with her small case, then takes the cake from the roof and gets in the passenger seat with it in her lap. I'm left with Mia, taking one last look at the house she would have grown up in. It's bittersweet. One day, she'll look back at her baby photos and ask why we have a different home than before. Perhaps someday, I'll tell her everything about the events with Daniel and Abby. When she's old enough, I might even explain that they're both serving life sentences, and it's unlikely she'll ever meet Daniel.

Until then, we have a life to be getting on with. I take Mia to the car, strap her into her seat, then begin the long journey back to London. I don't even look back at the house – I'm done with it, and I'm totally ready to start a new life with my baby girl.

There's just one stop I have to make along the way.

DANIEL IS AN INTELLIGENT MAN. There's no telling what Abby's intelligence was like, but I'll never know because she's gone from my life forever. She's living out her life in a different prison further away from here, while Daniel is stuck in the men's prison on the outskirts of Dolcester. That's where we park, ready for a final visit.

'Are you sure you don't want to take Mia with you?' Joanna asks.

'No, she can stay here. Keep her happy, will you?'

'Will it take long?'

'Not at all.'

I go to the back and kiss Mia on the head. She smiles as I take her and hand her to Joanna, who starts making her laugh with a series of duck noises. It's hard not to feel blessed as I walk into the prison, escorted by a guard to the visitors' section. The first thing I notice in here is the smell. It's like something stale. The air is cold in this stone fortress, everything looking clinical. I take a seat in a large room with eight tables spread out evenly. Nobody else is here save for another guard beside a door at the far end of the room. He nods at me, and I nod back, silently communicating either a hello or confirmation that I'm okay. I feel so small in this place, which isn't helped by the fact I'm swaddled in layers of baggy clothes.

The Sister-in-Law

While I wait for Daniel to come out, I consider how lucky I was to have caught him out. Not only did Joanna arrive in the nick of time that day, the police seeing him threaten to use a pistol, but Daniel and Abby never did ask for my phone. It was in my pocket the whole time they were discussing their plan, recording every word they said about the people they'd killed and what they intended to do to me. That phone is in evidence now, and good riddance.

It was just another reminder of the psycho who bought it for me in the first place.

The door clangs open, and Daniel is escorted to the table. He looks a wreck, his head shaved and his skin already so pale. The way he looks at me says he never expected to see me again, and if I were him, I wouldn't get used to it.

He takes a seat at the table, which I assume is deliberately sized for him to not reach me if he decides to lash out. I feel safe knowing he couldn't get to me without two guards rushing over and beating him to the ground. In fact, I almost wish he'd try.

It would be nice to see him in a little pain.

'What are you doing here?' he asks, his voice small and frail. It's like his confidence has vanished along with the act he always put up. It makes me wonder if he's a big fish inside the prison or if he has to perform... let's just say 'duties' for the other inmates.

'I came to say goodbye,' I tell him.

'Aww, you *do* care.'

'No, this is for my own sense of closure.'

Daniel sighs, glances around, then settles his stare on me again. 'Where's Mia?'

'Out in the car. Away from you.'

'Go and get her.'

'Not a chance.'

'Hey. If you're going to leave my life, at least let me see my daughter one last time.'

I shake my head defiantly, just slightly enjoying the sense of power I have over him. It was never my intention to use our baby as a weapon, but my self-confidence is repairing itself second by second. Besides, even if payback had nothing to do with it, I still wouldn't want to expose her to an environment like this.

'Are you even sorry?' I ask, changing the subject. 'About the things you did?'

'Why should I be? It's a dog-eat-dog world out there, no?'

'I suppose so. If that's your reasoning.'

'It certainly is. We do what we must in order to survive, Louise.' He sits back in his chair and crosses his arms. Gone is the upright posture of a professional doctor. Vacant is the demeanour of someone happy and proud. What I'm looking at now is nothing more than a killer. 'So, go on, get it over with.'

'Get what over with?'

'You came here to gloat, didn't you? To rub in the fact that I'm in here.'

'Not at all. Like I said, I just want closure.'

Daniel laughs. It's an eerie sound that sends a chill down my spine. 'Well, you're not getting any. See, someday, I *will* get out of here. We'll probably both be old, but mark my words: the very first thing I'll do is come and finish the job. Then I'll find Mia and tell her everything she knows is a lie. I'll say you framed me.'

'You'll lie to her? Even after all this?'

'Of course I will. I'll do anything to take my daughter back.'

I can't help it – I start to smile. The more I try to hide it, the wider it gets. The wider it gets, the more Daniel's starts to fade as confusion takes over. It's so clear that the last thing he expected was for me to start grinning like an idiot. It's written all over his lost expression, like there's a joke he's not privy to… and there is.

'What's so funny?' he says, balling his hands into fists.

'It's just that you keep saying she's your daughter.' I lean forward now, finally ready to let him in on a little secret I've been holding on to all this time – something I never intended to tell him, and now I simply can't help myself. 'But she's not yours. She never was.'

'What the hell are you talking about?'

My eyes meet his, and I let it all out. 'I had an affair, Daniel. You're not Mia's father.'

I TELL him everything about the man who fathered Mia. I tell him about how we used to meet for lunch and then go back to his house for some romance. I explain how we kept it a secret all this time. Daniel listens to me, looking as blown away as he should feel.

'It's nobody you know,' I say, looking for a sign of emotion in his eyes. 'His name is Martin, and we've been sleeping together for some time. It started as a one-off thing that neither of us could resist, but then it happened again and again. Before we knew it, we were meeting two or three times per week to spend a little time alone.

'When I got the news I was pregnant, the first thing I did was reach out to Martin. He insisted we get a DNA test done, so we did. He's the father, Daniel.' I lean in a little closer. 'Which means you'll never have a claim on her, and she hasn't inherited your lunatic genes.'

It happens in a split second. Daniel launches across the table, his hand reaching out for one last attack. I don't blame him for trying or for screaming at me as the guards drag him out of the room and back to his cell. It would hurt me, too, to learn that Mia isn't mine. But if anyone deserves to rot in a cell, helpless against the information he just acquired, it's him.

As for me? Well, perhaps I was lying when I said there was only one last stop before heading back to London. Because there is another place on the list, and it's not like I can avoid it. Martin deserves to meet his daughter at long last, so I leave the prison in the comfort of knowing I'll never see Daniel or Abby again. Mia and I are safe now.

Safe and free.

Chapter 32
Louise

WE STOP outside a beautiful house right on the very edge of Dolcester. It has four bedrooms and a drive big enough to fit four cars on. It's no wonder Martin can afford a place like this – he's been a very successful online marketer for many years now, and his finance is only growing with each year. If people knew I was cheating on Daniel this whole time, they might start suspecting me of having a type.

Wealthy.

But money has nothing to do with it. I simply fell in love with Daniel because I thought he was wonderful. Only later, when the cracks began to show, did I start seeking comfort in the arms of another man. I'd always tried to convince myself I had the perfect life, but that was simply a segue into someday ending things with Martin. It's not like I could go on living two separate lives. It had to end someday, which only got more complicated with the pregnancy.

'Are you sure you're ready for this?' Joanna asks, leaning out of the passenger seat to gawk up at the amazing house. 'You know, if you don't want him, tell him I'm single.'

I laugh awkwardly, absolutely petrified of what's about to happen. I'm not even sure how this is going to go – should I inform him that I'm officially a single woman and that now I'm available to be more than just a mistress? Maybe he won't want me, which is fine, but he definitely deserves a chance to be a father to his little girl. Mia will want that, too. In many years to come. I don't want either of them to miss out on a chance of bonding from a young age. They both deserve a lot more than that.

'You can do this,' Joanna says, sitting back and looking at me. 'You've gone through bigger things, and very recently. If you think you're not worthy of love, that's just a scar left by Daniel and his wicked woman.'

'But what if you're wrong?' The stress building up inside me is barely survivable. I'm just glad Mia is sleeping through this in her car seat. 'What if he's not interested in getting to know his own daughter?'

'Then you turn around and head straight back to the car.'

'And never see Martin again?'

'If that's what it takes, but honey, you're moving to London.'

She's right – this was never going to work out anyway. I haven't heard from Martin since things got rough back at home. The police investigation and news reports must have frightened him off, and I can't say I blame him. But I *do* miss him. It's now been almost three months, and it's getting harder to deal with his absence. There have been no messages, calls, or emails. I haven't even seen him in the village, which is particularly strange because he used to love drinking at the White Lion. I remember because it made things uncomfortable whenever Daniel and I would go there for lunch or dinner.

'I'm worthless,' I say defeatedly.

'Look at me,' Joanna says, and I do. 'Forget about the mistakes you made. Don't even worry about the fact you cheated on your husband. That's all stuff you can worry about later. For now, try to focus on the one important thing: letting that man meet his daughter.'

She's absolutely right. I've been selfish enough, not just by sleeping with Martin but by putting up a proverbial wall between him and his daughter. I did it because I was scared he would get too close – that Daniel would find out the truth and leave me. Now that it's not a problem, I can just own up to my mistakes and talk to Martin. That's all it will take: one small conversation. If he doesn't want to get involved, I'm certain he'll tell me.

I thank Joanna and exit the car, grateful to have her at my side. If we met under other circumstances, we probably wouldn't get along, but I owe her a debt. She saved my life by stopping Daniel from taking Mia away. I'll never stop being grateful for that, and what's more, I trust her wholly. So if she says I should go and talk to Martin, that's what I'll do.

It just starts with a single step.

EVEN FACTORING IN RECENT EVENTS, walking up to Martin's front door is one of the hardest things I've ever had to do. The closer I get to the house, the more convinced I am that this was a bad idea – that I should return to the vehicle, drive away, and never return.

There's a car on the drive, although I'm not sure what it is. It's not something I'd ever imagine Martin driving. He always liked sports cars, and that affinity for high-powered engineering kind of excited me. I guess he's something of a bad boy but one of the rare kinds that has his ducks in a row. It's like having the energy of a teenager and the behaviour of an adult.

But this car right here?

It's not very Martin.

When I'm almost at the front door, I have to ignore my flight reflex by turning to look at Joanna. She's giving me a very hard-to-see thumbs up from inside the car, which encourages me to keep going. Every time I think about how hard that incredible woman fought to bring Daniel and Abby to justice, it reminds me that I should strive to be that way, too. There's nothing quite like facing your fears, she keeps saying, so I push the doorbell and feel a surge of adrenaline as silhouettes start to move behind the stained glass.

Then he opens the door, looking as handsome as ever. He's olive-skinned and so cleanly shaved that he could easily pass for twenty-something. I'm dazzled by his boyish good looks all over again, immediately bowled over just like I was the very first time, when he flirted with me at the café and things got out of hand. It's hard to think that we were lovers only a short while ago. The man half hiding behind the door isn't the same person I spent many sneaky afternoons with between the sheets. His confidence is gone as he appears almost sheepish.

'Louise?' he says, looking me up and down as if I look different, too.

'Can we talk?' I ask. 'It's important.'

Martin leans out of the door, looking up and down the street. He only briefly glances at my new car, widens the door, and waves me in. As soon as I enter, I'm hit with a weird wave of nostalgic bliss. We've made love in this enormous hallway. Our clothes used to scatter over the wide, marble staircase as we made our way to the bedroom. Sometimes we didn't even get *that* far while we gave in to our animalistic senses on the upstairs landing.

But those days are gone. If it wasn't obvious from the awkward, bumbling way he's behaving, then it will soon become clear when I tell him I'm moving – that even if he wants to patch things up and try a real relationship, we can't.

Because he's staying right here.

'What brings you here?' he asks, not inviting me any further in than the hall. His hands are in the pockets of his perfectly pressed chinos, his back against the wall. 'I saw a lot about what happened on the news. I can't believe...'

'Yeah.' I nod, avoiding talk of all that. 'It's in the past.'

'Does he know about us?'

'I told him about half an hour ago.'

'What did he say?'

'Does it matter? We'll never see him again.'

Martin bobs his head up and down, his eyes glazing over as he stares at the floor and lets that sink in. When he's finally found a way to digest it, I can see it physically pains him to ask. 'And Mia? Is there something you need from me? Money, maybe?'

'No. No money. That's not what this is about.'

'What, then?'

'Mia and I are moving to London. Right now. She's going to ask about her father a lot in the coming years, and I thought you might want a chance to be a part of her life. Maybe introduce yourself or... I don't know. You could come with us.'

Martin sucks in a breath. 'I can't really do that.'

The floor falls out from under me. My world collapses. I already knew he wasn't the type to climb aboard the parenting ship, but I was hoping for *some* kind of interest. From the way Martin's shoulders rise with tension, it seems that won't be happening.

'May I ask why?'

'She was an accident, Louise.'

'She was a surprise to me, too. But she needs her parents.'

'Look, I'll send you money if you want it. There's plenty to go around. But I can't be a part of whatever arrangement you have going on. I never intended to be a dad – it was never in the plan. So thank you for coming to ask, but I have to decline. I'll make a lousy father anyway.'

I couldn't have said it better myself. It's not that I don't appreciate the offer of money, but I feel foolish for ever having been excited by a man such as this. It's probably what I deserve after cheating on my husband. But Mia deserves so much better.

Is a bad father better than no father?

We'll soon find out.

'Is there anything else?' he asks, business as usual.

I don't get time to answer before I'm cut off by the sound of a key in the front door. Martin leaps away from the wall and takes a couple of steps from me, distancing himself as if he's afraid of how it might look. When I see the stunning redhead come in with a bag of groceries, dumping her keys on the side and smiling at me through perfect ruby lipstick, I see why.

He's already replaced me with a full-time partner.

'Oh, who's this?' she asks more politely than she probably intended.

'This is Louise, an old friend.' Martin half escorts me out by putting a hand on my back and pressing gently to move me nearer the door. 'Louise, this is Bernice. She's my girlfriend, and if you haven't noticed already—'

'You're having a baby.' I'm not even angry when I spot the massive bump in her tummy. I just let out a small huff of a laugh and find a way to smile. So much for not being the father type. 'Congratulations,' I tell them both, trying to sound as happy for them as possible while pretending I haven't figured out the overlap.

It seems Martin is super-fertile.

'All right,' I sigh. 'I better get going. Nice to see you, Martin. And to meet you, Bernice.'

'Lovely meeting you!'

I'm already out of the door before she can finish her sentence, cutting her off just like she did to me. Martin closes the door within two seconds of me leaving, which gives me just enough time to hide the flood of tears. Mia won't have a father now. At least unless I happen to meet someone.

And that may never happen.

Our new life in London could work just fine.

It's been two weeks since we got here. We're completely unpacked in a lovely house, courtesy of Daniel's money and Joanna's help in getting us organised. It sounds corny, but she's already like a sister to me. The way she lights up when Mia plays with her is heart-warming. I wonder if it's her big-sister nature coming out.

She must miss Anita.

Mia is settling, too. She looks at the door every now and then though. She could be thinking about going out and exploring the big, wide world, or she could just be expecting Daniel to come home. She could be missing him badly – could be missing

Abby, too. That gets me thinking, with a quick flood of misery.

When will she call *me* Mama?

It's hard to say how things are going to go from here, but I have learned my lesson. No more putting myself under rich men who don't care about me. No more lies or betrayals. I want a good environment for my little girl to grow up in. I want her to know kindness, honesty, and loyalty. They're simple values that are hard to come by these days, but I'll always keep them at the forefront of my mind when I raise my daughter.

Maybe I'll learn a little something, too.

For other books by AJ Carter, visit:

www.ajcarterbooks.com/books

About the Author

AJ Carter is a psychological thriller author from Bristol, England. His first book, *The Family Secret*, is praised by critics around the world, and he continues to regularly deliver suspenseful novels you can't put down.

Sign up to his mailing list today and be the first to hear about upcoming releases and hot new deals for existing books. You'll also receive a FREE digital copy of *The Couple Downstairs* – an unputdownable domestic thriller you won't find anywhere else in the world.

www.ajcarterbooks.com/subscribe

Printed in Great Britain
by Amazon